HOW THINGS WORK IN FAERY

JOHN KRUSE

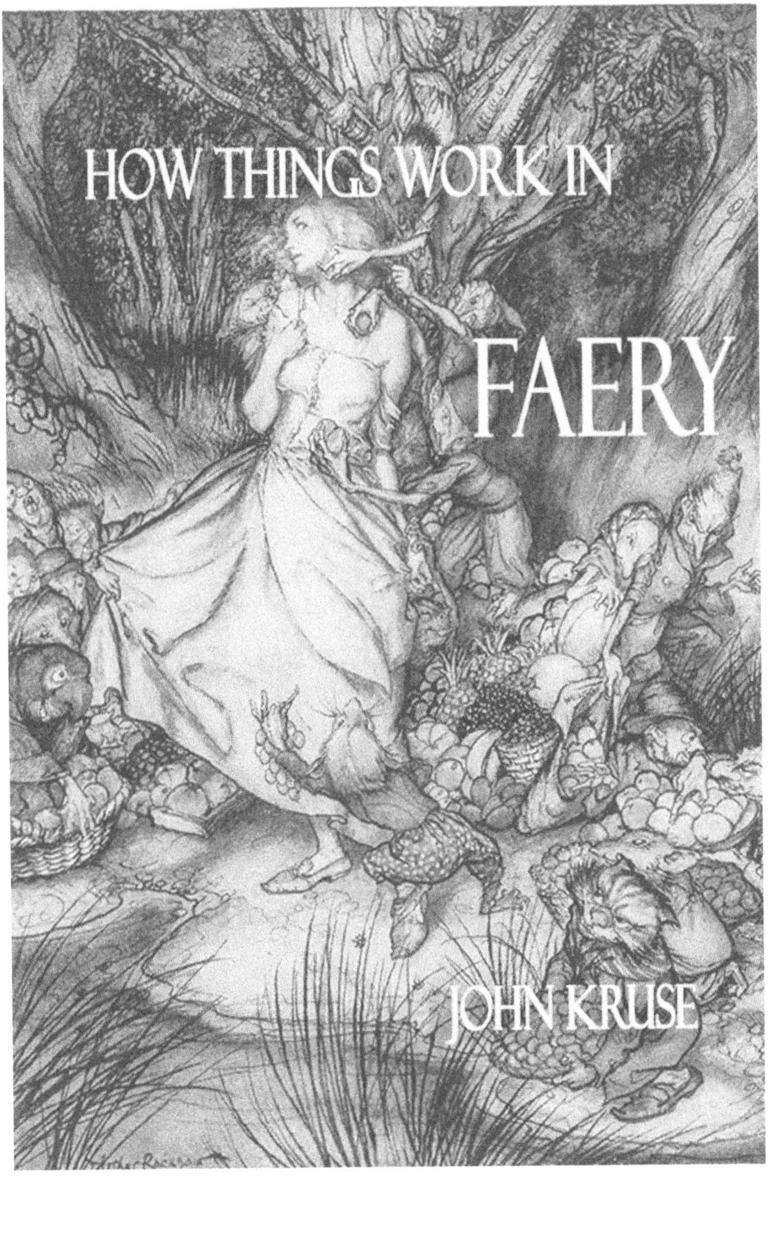

GREEN MAGIC

Green Magic

53 Brooks Road

Street

Somerset

BA16 0PP

England

www.greenmagicpublishing.com

Designed & typeset by K.DESIGN

Winscombe, Somerset

ISBN 9781838132460

GREEN MAGIC

Contents

Foreword

We regularly discuss the activities of fairies and their interactions with the human world, but far less often do we try to understand how their world functions in itself.

By concentrating on the fairies' impact upon the physical world that we know, we are guilty of being very self-centred, and of viewing fairies as solely significant in so far as they have some influence upon our own affairs. They are, of course, a separate universe (we might sometimes say kingdom, but this is too narrow) and within their world there is a rich complexity of organisation and creativity.

This book pulls together everything we know about how things work in Faery. The information is scattered across many narratives, but once it is assembled, we discover we have a detailed picture of their politics and economy. Much of this is entirely independent of human affairs. It is true to say that they often intermeddle in mankind's activities – often stealing and disrupting, sometimes sharing and giving – but their societies are capable of functioning perfectly well without our input. In fact, we have learned much from them – and fairy examples and fairy influence can sometimes be detected in our own affairs, as I will show.

On their Character and Manners

By way of preface to what follows, I shall offer some general observations on the attitudes and expectations of the denizens of Faery.

Let me begin with a warning, whose implications will run like a thread throughout the rest of the book. This is: those who dwell in Faery will never regard mortals as equal partners, whether it be in trade, in personal interactions or even in romantic connections. The mortal is always regarded as the inferior party in these encounters – and the sooner we humans acknowledge and accept such an imbalance in our dealings, the sooner shall we adjust our expectations, be on our guard and be reconciled to our treatment.

First in every fairy's calculations is the benefit of himself and his kind. We should never mistake gifts for kindness or generosity for love. In their estimation, we are very like pets: it pleases them to indulge us but they feel no obligation to be constant in their affections nor consistent in their conduct. They help because it pleases them; but if their amusement wanes, their attitude can change.

Faeries are strict in their expectations of mortals. Their keen sense of propriety and good order, their high standards for lovers, housekeepers and for those assisting them are well known. We should never demand reciprocity; the obligations flow all one way. Don't expect them to act towards you in the same way that they insist you behave towards them.

Lastly, discreteness is all. They may be very ready to trade, to dispense good fortune or even to engage in love, but in all such interrelations, the strictest secrecy is demanded. The lucky recipient of their favour should never presume to think that this good fortune should be shared with other mortals less lucky than themselves. Disclosure of any such dealings with faeryland is the surest and most certain way to their termination.

Fairy Resources

The basis of any economy is, of course, to be found in the resources available to nation in question. The fairy commonwealth has many traits in common with human polities – as well as some unique sources of wealth.

POPULATION

What can be achieved by a country depends very much upon the numbers of citizens resident and economically active there. Regrettably, we lack any census of the fairy population, so that it is impossible to estimate with any sense of accuracy how many productive and non-productive denizens it comprises. All that can be said is that, from the evidence of human experience, fairies are spread throughout Britain and, it may be added, throughout the world, so that the indications are that there are numbers of people perhaps comparable to the pre-industrial and pre-urban population figures for the human world. In other words, there would seem to be enough active adults to be productive, self-sustaining and have an active commerce in goods and materials.

Even if there were deficiencies in numbers, the fairies have a solution to that. As will be discussed in a later chapter, they actively supplement their numbers (both adult and infant) by taking humans into their world. These additions to their workforce make up for any lack of numbers or of skills they may suffer.

FAIRY LAND

The greatest resource for any nation is its land. Fairyland is generally invisible to us, either because it is concealed by fairy glamour or because it is substantially situated below the ground, which makes it hard to estimate acreages, but what evidence we have indicates that it is just as productive as any human land.

According to the twelfth century chronicler Geoffrey of Wales, Welsh boy Elidyr ran away from the punishments of his tutor and met some little men by a river bank. They led him down a dark passage to a beautiful country, adorned with "rivers, meadows, woods and plains." From this description it's clear that an abundant water supply, timber and grazing for livestock all exist in Faery.[1]

Other much more recent accounts underline this impression. A man called Richard Vingoe, wandering in a cave in cliffs near Land's End, eventually came upon a "pleasant looking country" and the famous Green Children, who strayed out of Faery into twelfth century Suffolk, had been tending their father's flocks of sheep in the fields.[2] In the tale of *Sir Orfeo*, the visitors to fairyland witnessed:

---

1   Gerald of Wales, *Journey Through Wales*, Book I, chapter 8.
2   Bottrell, *Hearthside Stories*, vol.2, 102; Ralph of Coggeshall, *Chronicon Anglicanum*.

"Rivers, forestes, frith (glades) with flours,
  And his riche stedes (places) ichon."
"He com into a fairy cuntray...
  Smothe and plain and al greene,
  Hille no dale was there non ysene."

In *Orfeo,* the King of Fairies' realm is both level and productive. It's an ideal landscape of almost perfect fertility.

The Welsh story of *Einion and Olwen* tells of how a boy descends by a long staircase under a large boulder until he reaches "a fine wooded, fertile country... The bright waters of rivers meandered in twisted streams, and the hills were covered with the luxuriant verdure of their grassy growth, and the mountains with a glossy fleece of smooth pasture."[3]

This too sounds like a rich and fertile land, as Thomas of Erceldoune was also able to testify:

"Scho lede hym intill a faire herbere (orchard),
  Whare frute was growand gret plentee;
  Pere and appill both rype thay were,
  The date, and als the damasee (damson);
  The fygge, and also the wyneberye;"

It was not just gardens and orchards that were fruitful. In about 1150 (or earlier) a swineherd at Peveril Castle in Derbyshire lost one of his sows and searched for it in one of the caves that lies under the limestone hills of the Peak District. After much walking, he came to a bright place where reapers were gathering in the harvest.

---

3   Rhys, *Celtic Folklore,* Oxford: Clarendon Press, 1901, 112.

The accumulated evidence, then, indicates that there is fertile and extensive farming land in Faery. For better or for worse, however, fairies aren't solely reliant upon the productivity of their own lands.

FAERY GROUND

Land on the earth surface is also cultivated by the fairies and, in fact, it may even be granted to them deliberately by human communities. In Gloucestershire, presumably valuable agricultural land was given up to the fairies: when the fields at Upton St Leonard's were enclosed, an area called No Nation was left for the faeries' use and tall trees were left in the new hedgerows as places in which the fays could hide.[4]

In the same way in Berwickshire, on the Scottish border with England, there's a tradition of preserving areas called Clootie's Craft (or croft) and Goodman's Field, that were set aside in villages for the fairies and were never tilled or cropped by humans. It was considered extremely unlucky to dig or plough on these portions, for:

"He who tills the fairies' green
Nae luck again shall hae."

It was said that, "If you put a spade in the Goodman's craft… [the Devil] will shoot you with his shaft." Another rhyme, composed to warn locals against reckless cultivation, advised farmers that:

---

4   R. Palmer, *Folklore of Gloucestershire,* Stroud: Tempus, 2001, 145.

"The craft lies bonny by Langton Lees
  And is well liked by birds and bees.
  If you plough it up, it'll be your death,
  For disturbing the sod where the fairies like to tread."[5]

Fields that are ploughed by the fairies have been identified in several parts of Britain. Whether they are these specially reserved sites or other areas of land that they have appropriated is not clear, but both on the Scottish Isle of Arran and in Northumberland, in the north of England, 'elf-furrows' can be seen in the landscape where the fairies have ploughed arable land in the past.[6]

Generally, then, it was accepted by human farmers that there were areas of land that were the rightful property of fairies and that trespasses upon these were ill-advised. In his poem *The Faithful Shepherdess,* John Fletcher recognised this:

"Then, boldly here, where we shall ne'er be found,
  No Shepherd's way lies here; this hallowed ground:
  No maid seeks here her strayed cow or sheep,
  Fairies and fawns, and satyrs, do it keep."

Likewise, John Aubrey recalled being told by Elias Ashmole that there was a piper in Lichfield who knew which houses in the town stood on fairy ground – and that he had often seen the Good Folk there. It's because of such a presence that the

---

5   G. Henderson, *Popular Rhymes... of the County of Berwick,* Newcastle: W S Crow, 1856, 111.
6   McArthur, *Antiquities of Arran,* Edinburgh: Adam, Charles & Black, 1873, 69; Doel, *Folklore of Northumberland,* Stroud: The History Press Ltd, 2009, 18.

character Leon, in John Fletcher's play *Rule a Wife and Have a Wife,* questions whether or not his house may "stand on fairy ground? We're haunted." In such cases as these, some sharing presumably was tolerated. At Lonan on the Isle of Man, there was an example of a 'Fairy House' (*Thie Ferrishyn*) which was the first or oldest dwelling in a village. The local fairies would be fondest of this and spend more time there than in any other residence in the place. Fairy music and other noises were sometimes heard coming from the Lonan cottage. Such cases of peaceful co-existence are, however, rare, as we shall see.[7]

For a race generally regarded as aethereal and otherworldly, the fairies are surprisingly proprietorial and protective of their land. They have frequently been known to take active steps to deal with human trespasses, 'abating the nuisance' through self-help means as English lawyers would say. Buildings to which the fairies object because they are constructed in places which the fairies regard as their own are frequently moved to another location, whether that happens during the building process or once the structure is complete. Glamis Castle was repeatedly demolished overnight when building work started, with the materials being thrown off a cliff; more often the stones and timber are carried to a site deemed more suitable, as on Guernsey, where the materials and tools for Castel Church were moved three times before the builders finally accepted the new spot chosen for the church by the faeries. Across Britain, churches are the buildings most

---

7   Fletcher, *The Faithful Shepherdess,* 1608-9; Aubrey, *Remains of Gentilisme,* London: Folklore Society, 1881, 125; Fletcher, *Rule a Wife,* 1624, Act V, scene 3; see too Drayton, *Nymphidia,* stanza 9: "so called Fayrie ground,/ Of which they have the keeping;" Gill, *Second Manx Scrapbook,* 95–6.

commonly relocated to new sites, perhaps because the faes object to the purpose of the building as much as to the place chosen.[8] In Berwickshire, the local faeries tried to remove Langton House to Dogden Moss, but as they started to take the building apart, the occupier awoke and cried out "Lord keep me!" – thereby driving the attackers off. This man was very lucky. A cottage built at Glencallum on Bute somehow offended the Good Folk and they carried it off whole with the people inside. All that was ever found again was the door lintel, which had fallen in Bransar Bog.[9]

Mostly, it looks as though these actions are motivated by the fairies' objections to infringements of their property rights, but the removal of churches may indicate a moral aspect as well. This certainly seems to be the major motivation in an incident recorded at Inchdairnie in Fife. During the 1880s, an old woman living locally recalled that a "heinous crime" (we aren't told exactly what) was committed at a house there. Because this was viewed by the fairies as a violation of their land and, moreover, land upon which their sacred oaks stood, they demolished the building in a single night. Attempts were made to rebuild by the owner, but the work was undone every night until it was abandoned.[10]

---

8   J. Cargill Guthrie, *The Vale of Strathmore*, 1875, 35; E. MacCulloch, *Guernsey Folklore*, 1903, 221.
9   G. Henderson, *Popular Rhymes... of the county of Berwick*, 1856, 68; J. Hewison, *The Isle of Bute in Olden Time*, vol.1, 1893, 56.
10 J. Wilkie, *Bygone Fife, North of the Lomonds*, 1938, 14.

Fairy Productivity

We are inclined to imagine fairies as pastoral and anti-mechanical beings, wandering free of cares in flowery meadows. A large part of this imagery comes from Shakespeare and other Renaissance British poets, who wrote much about Colin, Chloris and nymphs. At the same time, as we shall see, there is plentiful evidence in opposition to this image, which instead shows the fairies to be active farmers as well as being miners and metalworkers.

FLEEING INDUSTRY?

Confusingly, the faes are reputed to flee human agricultural and manufacturing activity. There's a widespread rhyme in Scotland to the effect that:

> "Where the scythe cuts and the sock (plough) rives,
> Hae done wi' fairies and bee-bykes."

This couplet indicates that intensive arable farming repels the fays, something confirmed by an account from Menstrie, in Clackmannanshire, which blamed modern agrarian methods and commercial enterprise: the fairies fled "stone fences, cotton mills and the copse destroying plough."[11]

Crop raising by humans wasn't the only source of faery discontent, however. Evans Wentz in the 1900s heard in Scotland that the Highland clearances also drove off the *sith*. Highlander John Dunbar of Invereen told him that "no one sees them now because every place on this parish where they used to appear has been put into sheep and deer and grouse and shooting." A vision of them fighting with sheep had been seen before the population was cleared, in fact, as a premonition of what was to follow.[12]

Moreover, it's not just the growing of food to which the faeries object, apparently, but processing the produce too. For example, on the Isle of Man, when the steam flour mill was built at Colby, the local fairies gave up their former haunts in its vicinity. Early one morning they were seen climbing up into the mists and solitude of the mountain glens, lamenting loudly and with their household goods on their backs.[13] Likewise, the railways: describing the Isle of Man in 1874, Henry Irwin Jenkinson worried that the advent of railways and tourists (and, for that matter, Primitive Methodist chapels) meant that "the last haunts of the good people will be invaded and they will have to move elsewhere."[14]

This fear of modern mechanised transport expelling the supernatural residents had in fact been expressed as early as the 1840s, when a correspondent of *Notes and Queries* had

---

11 *County Folklore* vol.7, 315.
12 Evans Wentz, *Fairy Faith in Celtic Countries,* Oxford: Oxford University Press, 1911, 94.
13 Waldron, *Isle of Man,* Douglas: Manx Society, 1731, fn.56.
14 Jenkinson, *Practical Guide,* London: E. Stanford, 1874, 75 & 106.

worried that the railways would expel the fairies from "Merry England." It's said too that Glenshee in Perthshire was once full of fairies, but the arrival of steam whistles (whether on locomotives or factories is not clear) drove them away. The establishment of a linen factory at Catfirth on Shetland in the late eighteenth was reputed to have driven away the local trows.[15] It was also reported that, whilst the glaistig of Glen Duror had always avoided human houses, she quit the area entirely once steamers appeared on Loch Linnhe and blasting started in the new quartz quarry.[16]

Very similar accounts were heard from Wales in the last quarter of the nineteenth century. For example, "Fairies went out of Wales, my child, when the railroads came into it. Steam engines and electric telegraphs have played sad havoc with our old beliefs." The fairies fled, ever westward, in the face of advancing tracks and wires. In 1904, it was confirmed that Glamorgan had been cleared of its fairy residents by the smoke, noise and bustle of collieries, ironworks and railways. It's fair to add, though, that encroaching industry wasn't identified as the sole culprit. Methodism and teetotalism were also indicted, with one old parishioner even complaining that it was tea drinking that had driven the fair folk away.[17]

---

15 *Notes & Queries*, vol.9, 1860, 259; Evans Wentz, 86; J. Nicolson, *Shetland Folklore*, London: R. Hale, 1981, 84.

16 MacDougall & Calder, *Folk Tales and Fairy Lore in Gaelic and English*. Edinburgh: John Grant, 1910, 267.

17 *Cardiff Times*, December 26th 1874, 3– 'The Welsh Harper & The Fairies;' *Rhondda Leader*, Sept.17th 1904, 7– 'Gossiping Notes;' *The Welshman*, October 22nd 1858, 8– 'Tea & Fairies.' See too *Bradford Observer*, October 6th 1842, 7 'Observers' Club–' steam engines had driven fairies out of Scotland whilst in England telegraphs and railways were to blame: *North Wales Chronicle & Advertiser*, July 29th 1880, 7– 'Elves & Goblins.'

All of the foregoing would seem strongly to indicate the anti-industrial, anti-commercial nature of faery society. This tendency has been accelerated since the 1960s: our own sense of environmental degradation and of worsening climate change has emphasised for us the green aspects of faery nature.

FAERY INDUSTRY

And yet – the faeries have been known regularly to use human water mills to grind their own flour. There is even a record of a mill operated by the local fairies on a commercial basis at Cleitinn, outside Pitlochry, in mid-Scotland. Likewise, in a small tarn next to Loch Lomond, there was once said to be a fairy operating a cloth dyeing business. It was not highly commercial, it's true, as he only requested small gifts rather than formal payment for his work, but he nonetheless expected to be fairly treated and fairly paid. When a shepherd asked for a black fleece to be dyed white, the fairy felt his skill was being abused and, in anger, he tipped all his dyes in the tarn and abandoned the site forever.[18]

Equally, despite the fays' alleged aversion to steam power, we also have a bizarre and contrary story from the south of Man. Fairies were seen operating a railway on moonlit nights – twenty years before the first actual track was laid along the same route. This vision seems to be a manifestation of the fairies' power to see the future and their tendency to convey that knowledge to us by acting it out. Even so, it is a little odd

---

18 Dixon, *Pitlochry Past & Present,* Pitlochry: L. Mackay, 1925, 133; H. Winchester, *Traditions of Arrochar and Tarbert,* 1916.

that they should want to pass this information in this manner, if they objected so vehemently to the outcome.[19]

Furthermore, the involvement of the fays with mechanical transport is a trend that has begun to emerge distinctly in more recent reports of sightings. Obviously, the fairies have no need of modern technology, but they seem to like to appear with it, all the same. Most famous is the 'Wollaton incident' at Nottingham in 1979, when a number of little men were seen driving around a park in hovering cars. Some girls in Cornwall in the 1940s woke one night and saw a small gnome-like man driving a tiny red car in circles outside their house. In 1929 two young children in Hertford witnessed a fairy flying a biplane over their garden.[20]

As well as these motor vehicles, there appears to be a developing fairy fascination with machinery. Marjorie Johnson records cases of fairies drawn to type-writers and sewing machines, as well as an incident when some 'leprechauns' diagnosed a fault in a bus engine.[21]

It is easy to fall back on the excuse that the fairies are 'contrary' and that they can demonstrate diametrically opposed traits at the same time, but we probably have to do better at explaining the evidence than this. We know that they are generally secretive people, and part of their response to industrialisation must be born of an aversion to the encroaching spread of human influence. We know too of them fleeing the noise and clamour of the human world. This began early, with a dislike of church bells (for which stories come from Exmoor and Worcestershire), so a desire to escape

---

19 Gill, *Second Manx Scrapbook*, c.3.
20 see Janet Bord, *Fairies*, New York: Carroll & Graf, 1997, 73–76.
21 *Seeing Fairies*, 101 & 322–2.

modern mechanical noise is entirely predictable. For instance, when the mill at Kiondroghad on the Isle of Man was run overnight one time, the fays threw a broom at the millers in warning. They may have disliked the noise – but they might just as well have been objecting to what they regarded as their rightful evening use of the mill being disturbed.[22]

SUMMARY

It appears that the faeries aren't against manufacture or cultivation as such. To some degree, double standards are probably at work, with activities disliked when humans perform them which would have raised no complaint if the faeries had been involved. Their interests and their convenience are always their first considerations. Be that as it may – the fairies are curious and they are prepared to move with the times. They will adopt human innovations if it suits or amuses them. In general, though, they appear to prefer less intensive modes of production – more handicraft as against mass manufacture, more traditional forms of cultivation as against mechanised farming. We might venture to say that they are more likely to be organic and low impact in their approach – something that fuels the modern conception of them being 'eco-guardians.'

---

22 Gill, *Second Manx Scrapbook*, c.III.

Faery Governance and the Faery State

If the mother of trade and prosperity is peace, their midwife must be dominion. Stability and security are vital for confidence in secure exchange, but the greater a nation that a ruler controls, and the more numerous the population and the products of that land, the greater the market for commodities.

English author Maurice Hewlett, in his 1913 novel *The Lore of Proserpine*, questioned the nature of faery governance. He asked "are we to understand that any kind of Government resembling that of human societies obtains among them? When we talk of Kings or Queens of the Fairies, of Oberon and Titania, for example, are we using a rough translation of a real something, or are we telling the mere truth?" Hewlett carried on to question the exact status of Queen Mab, the Lady of the Lake, and of folk titles like 'Mistress of the Wood' and 'Lady of the Hill.' He himself referred in his stories to the 'King of the Wood,' an evocative title but one that seems to have been borrowed from Roman legend by way of Fraser's *The Golden Bough*. As Hewlett recognised, many of the kings and queens whose names we know come from romance, not from faery lore. Hewlett concluded that the fairies lacked leaders and royal families. Even so, they recognise the authority of greater spirits but, in essence, theirs is an anarchy: "The fairies are of a world where

Right and Wrong don't obtain, where Possible and Impossible are the only finger-posts at cross-roads; for the gods themselves give no moral sanction to desire and hold up no moral check." We should remind ourselves, even so, that his conception of Faery was his own unique blend of Greek myth and British folklore and cannot be regarded as an authentic reflection of popular understanding of how their world is organised.[23]

FAIRY MONARCHY

It is generally accepted that Faery is divided into separate polities subject to the rule of kings and queens.[24] Fairy monarchs have been reported in romance and ballads from the early Middle Ages onwards. In *Huon of Bordeaux*, for example, King Arthur is identified as the rightful heir to the realm of Oberon and in *Brune de la Montaigne*, he is described as 'lord of all fairy-haunted spots.'[25]

The fairy monarchy continued to appear in the plays and verse of the sixteenth century – for instance, Scot Montgomerie wrote of "the King of Pharie with the court of the Elph-quene." Later, in the late seventeenth century, fairy lore expert the Reverend Robert Kirk recorded that the fairies "are distributed in Tribes and Orders" and that they have "aristocraticall Rulers and Laws." Nineteenth century Scottish poet William Aytoun better reflected the Presbyterian view

---

23 M. Hewlett, *The Lore of Proserpine*, (New York: Charles Scribner, 1913), 'A Summary Chapter.'
24 For a modern literary manifestation of this, see Sylvia Townsend Warner's *Kingdoms of Elfin*.
25 See too *King Herla, King Berdok, Sir Orfeo, Thomas of Erceldoune* and Chaucer's *Sir Thopas*.

of the Scottish Church when he stated that "The queen of fairyland was a kind of feudatory sovereign under Satan, to whom she was obliged to pay kane or tithe in kind." This tithe was rendered in human souls – but this is very much a late and partisan stance.[26]

Kirk takes us far closer to the true folk belief than does the output of court poets (and most other priests) and it's very worthwhile considering the accounts given by Scottish witch trial suspects for the picture they paint of the court of Elphame. It's notable, nevertheless, that the bulk of these accounts come from the Lowland zone of Scotland. The Highlanders seemed less inclined to identify monarchs, but rather individuals equivalent, perhaps, to clan chiefs. For example, Donald McIlmichall of Inverary, when he was examined in 1677, mentioned "ane old man as seemed to have preference above the rest" and who "seemed to be chief, being ane large tall corporal Gardman." Kirk's parishes lay just on the edge of the Highland zone and his reference to an aristocracy rather than royalty may reflect this cultural as well as physical divide.[27]

Many of those accused of witchcraft confirm the hierarchical and monarchical arrangements already described. John Stewart of Irvine claimed he had made weekly visits to the fairy court; Isobel Gowdie was favoured with gifts of meat (food) by the monarchs and commented upon their fine clothes: the 'Qwein of Fearrie' was "brawlie clothed in whyt linens, and white and browne cloathes" and her husband was

---

26 Montgomerie, *Flyting Between Montgomerie & Polwart*, 1515 (and see too Lyndesay, *Complaynt of the Papago*); *Secret Commonwealth*, chapters 2 & 7; Aytoun cited in Simpson, *Folklore in Lowland Scotland*, 97.

27 MacPhaill, *Highland Papers*, Edinburgh: T. and A. Constable for the Scottish History Society, vol.III, 36–38.

a "braw man, weill favoured." Isobel Watson was privileged enough to be midwife to the fairy queen whereas Alison Pearson, from St Andrews in Fife, did not enjoy such access. Instead, she had (deceased) relatives present in the fairy court who were on good terms with the queen, she confessed to her trial in 1588, but she had never met her majesty, who was, by all accounts, quite moody. Sometimes she was good, sometimes evil; sometimes she was present in the court and sometimes elsewhere.[28]

Lastly, the ballad of *Tam Lin* backs up much of this preceding information. It describes, intriguingly, a three-fold structure within the 'elphin court.' In the case of the fairy queen who has abducted Tom Lin, she is accompanied on her Halloween faery rade by three separate groups of courtiers. The last, which rides with the queen and is dressed in robes of green, is the "head court of them all."[29]

What is especially striking from a number of the witch-trial accounts is the familiarity and down to earth nature of the fairy queen. Andro Man of Aberdeen met her when he was young and she had come to his home to give birth because his mother was a midwife. There and then, the queen promised to teach him healing and prophetic skills in return for the assistance he'd given that day during her labour. Elizabeth Dunlop from Lyne near Peebles was endowed with the same knowledge by the queen herself. This everyday contact went even further in some cases. Both Andro Man and Margaret Alexander of Livingston claimed sexual relations with the queen and king respectively; Alexander told the court in 1647

---

28 Pitcairn, *Ancient Criminal Trials in Scotland,* vol.3, Part 2, 602; vol.1, Part 3, 161.
29 *Child Ballad* 39D.

that her affair had gone on for thirty years and Man alleged that the relationship had produced "diverse bairns" over the space of thirty-two years.[30]

Bessie Dunlop was also visited in her own home by the queen, who looked to her like any ordinary middle-aged woman, stout and in need of a glass of beer. The most extreme example of the ordinariness of fairy royalty is probably the story of Angus Mór of Tomnahurich. He was told by a fairy that the only way to save his wife and child from abduction 'under the hill' was to be able to tell the fairy queen's secret on the bridge of Easan Dubh. At the appointed hour, he was on the bridge, where he heard a woman singing. Looking over the parapet, he saw the queen in the river below, doing her washing on a rock in the stream and singing the song that comprised her secret. The same collection of Gaelic stories includes one from Lochranza on the Isle of Arran, in which the fairy queen is seen in a harvest field in the shape of a large pregnant yellow frog. Her Majesty plainly was not one for airs and graces.[31]

In contrast to these prosaic accounts, the ballad of 'The Wee Wee Man' describes the fairy court in much more impressive terms: "Though the King of Scotland had been there/ The warst o them might hae been his queen." This suggests the power and wealth that we might be inclined to expect from a magical court.

Lastly, it is noteworthy that none of these monarchs are named. The Scottish witch suspects only ever met with or heard

---

30   *Spalding Club Miscellany,* vol.1, Part 3, 120; A. Macdonald, 'A Witchcraft Case of 1647,' *Scots Law Times,* April 10th, 1937, 77.

31   MacDougall & Calder, *Folk Tales & Fairy Lore,* 133; Robertson, 'Folklore from the West of Ross-shire,' *Transactions of the Gaelic Society of Inverness,* vol.26, 1905, 271.

talk of 'the fairy queen.' No personal names were disclosed (and the same is true in medieval verse romances such as *King Herla* or *Sir Orfeo*). There may be several explanations for this: it may be that faery royalty are so exalted that none may speak their names in any situation. It may be that it was not considered seemly for a human to be vouchsafed such precious knowledge and, given the magic power believed to inhere in fairy names, this could make considerable sense. It may be (and this concurs with some of the other evidence we have) that – in direct contradiction of what has just been suggested – the role is not considered to be so mighty nor so distinguished as to justify the usage of phraseology such as Queen X or His Majesty King Y. Rather, the position might have been temporary and much less exalted: the ruler was more of a manager or senior officer within the state who would be known by their job title – "the boss" or "the chief," in other words.

As many readers will be well aware, we do – of course – know some fairy monarchs' names. The truth is, however, that none of these should be regarded as authentic fairy names; they all appear to be human inventions applied as romantic labels to invented characters. Queen Mab is often regarded as an authentic fairy goddess queen. In some respects, she is, but the name derives from Irish myth and comes from the name Medb – the later forms of which are Meadhbh, Méabh and also Maeve – who is the Queen of Connacht in the Ulster Cycle. In origin, she is more likely to have been a goddess of sovereignty than a member of the good folk. Next, we may think of Shakespeare's Oberon. This king is, in fact, not the playwright's invention but was borrowed from medieval French romance, *Huon of Bordeaux*, which in turn took the royal name from Germanic legend. 'Oberon' is the French pronunciation of the Middle High German name *Alberic*, which is in turn nothing more than a description, for it simply means Elf King (*albe ric*). Finally, we must consider Oberon's spouse in *A Midsummer Night's Dream,* Titania. Once again, Shakespeare did not invent this name, but neither did he take it from British folklore. The name is Graeco-Roman, an epithet of the goddess Diana. She was often seen as Goddess of the Moon and Night Creatures and was equated with native supernaturals. 'Titania' means 'daughter of Titans', emphasising her origins in classical myth.

All our royal names, therefore, are borrowed from more or less far afield. The kings and queens of British faery are uniformly anonymous, a curious fact that should not be overlooked when assessing the extent and nature of their powers.

FAERY HIERARCHY

In her book, *A New Dictionary of Fairy,* Morgan Daimler remarked that "Fairy is a very feudal system... everything is tied together with debts and obligations and what's owed to who." Just what do we know about the hierarchy of fairy society beneath its monarch?[32]

The human societies of the High Middle Ages were, indeed, feudal, in that land was granted in return for services within a rigidly hierarchical and monarchic social structure, from the king down to the lowliest knight. The system was pyramidal, with the ruler overseeing a multitude of tenants and subtenants across each realm.

---

32 Morgan Daimler, *A New Dictionary of Fairy – A 21st Century Exploration of Celtic and Related Western European Fairies,* 2020, 120.

How closely does faery resemble this? We know of fairy kings and queens, obviously, and we know too of the importance of promises and obligations on fairy relationships. However, so far as we know, land – and rights over it – form no part of fairy social dynamics and the fairy hierarchy seems to be very flat – perhaps no more than two levels, comprising the monarch and subjects.

So far as we can tell, British fairy monarchs reigned over no highly structured nation nor over any court in which precedence or rank dominated. Fairy kings and queens were remarkably free of airs and graces. They undertook the most menial chores for themselves – so, for example, the elf king in the ballad *Sir Cawline* fights his own duels and does not rely on a champion. These kings and queens were not averse to entering sexual relationships with the humblest of humans either. Margaret Alexander, from Livingston in Scotland, told her 1647 witchcraft trial that the fairy king had taken her as his partner and, even, "laye with her upone the brige" at Linton. A monarch who appears ready to have open air sex in front of several of his subjects cannot be one who sees himself as very lofty and special.

Sometimes, intermediaries with the human world might be employed, as was the case with Thom Reid, who communicated with Bessie Dunlop on behalf of the fairy queen, but any more elaborate organisation than this seems to have been absent. The only exception to this statement is the system of multiple 'elphin courts' that's mentioned in some versions of the ballad of *Tam Lin*.[33] In verse two, we read of three courts including a 'head court' that is dressed in green and accompanies the queen. In the third rendering,

---

33   Child versions D, K & G.

the ranking is more complex, as Tam explains to his human
lover, Margret:

> "Then the first an court that comes you till
> Is published king and queen;
> The next an court that comes you till,
> It is maidens monyane.
> The next an court that comes you till
> Is footmen, grooms and squires;
> The next an court that comes you till
> Is knights, and I'll be there."

In this scheme, we have a very distinct and strict social ordering.
Usually, though, the most we hear of is some servants, as in the
ballad of *Leesom Brand,* in which the hero goes to the fairy
court aged ten to act as a server at the king's table. Of course,
such domestic servants were once quite common in a range of
households, and implied no great wealth or status.

Faery society is a very flattened pyramid, therefore, and
individual citizens have an almost compete autonomy it
seems. Perhaps the problem is that we lack any adequate
word to transliterate the fairy term: as mentioned, Donald
McIlmichael, tried at Inverary in 1674, said that he had seen
an old man inside the fairy hill he visited who "seemed to have
preference above the rest" and "seemed to be chief." Perhaps
there is seniority, priority and respect, but little more than that.

Nevertheless, regardless of the parties, interpersonal
relationships are governed by reciprocity. Good deeds should
always be repaid, and to the same degree or value. If a fairy
loans you some flour, always give exactly the same quality and
quantity back. Debts are remembered and will be exacted,

even decades later. It will be obvious that you should never enter into any sort of deal with the fairies unless you are able and willing to fulfil your side. Default is not an option, whatever level of faery society you may be transacting with.

FAE WARFARE

Whilst opinion is consistent that faery is ruled by a few individuals, there is next to no evidence on the number, size nor location of these monarchs' kingdoms. Is there a single realm or many within the island of Britain? We do not know, but the partial information we have on fairy armies and fairy battles supports the supposition that there are numerous warring tribes or polities. This would not be in the least surprising given reports of endemic violence from Ireland and Brittany.[34]

The Reverend Kirk is explicit on this aspect of fairy politics. He states that the fairy men have "many disastrous Doings of their own, as Convocations, Fighting, Clashes, Wounds and Burialls, both in the Earth and Air." They have weapons, made of stone rather than iron, and with these they resolve their differences. As he repeats, "These Subterraneans have Controversies, Doubts, Disputes, Feuds and Siding of Parties..." There seems very little scope for uncertainty here: faery is just as riven by dissension, greed and ambition as the human world and the males are as prone to rely on their strength of arms to settle these differences and, we can infer, to gain more land and greater wealth. All of this necessarily

---

34   see Evans Wentz, *Fairy Faith*, 44, 46, 50, 55, 57, 74, 207 & 211.

implies, in turn, that there will be military specialists within faery society.[35]

FAIRY SOLDIERS

Fairies are often described as looking like soldiers in eighteenth and nineteenth century British sources. For example, an old Cornish woman quoted by Robert Hunt compared them to "little sodgers." We should not, however, be misled by these accounts. All they're really telling us is that the beings sighted were wearing red (and possibly green) jackets; British soldiers at this time were, of course, called the 'red coats' and provided a ready analogy for witnesses.[36]

From time to time, nonetheless, armed fays have been sighted. The trows on Shetland have sometimes been spotted wearing armour. A boy abducted by the fairies on Islay in exchange for a changeling was eventually freed by his blacksmith father and returned home; it transpired that he had learned how to forge swords whilst he was away "under the hill." Lastly, at the opposite end of the country a host of spriggans encountered by smugglers on the beach of Mounts Bay at Eastern Green, just outside Penzance, were armed with bows and arrows, spears and slings and were organised in rank and file with marching music provided by pipes, cymbals and tambourines.[37]

---

35 *Secret Commonwealth,* chapters 6, 8 & 11.
36 For example, Hunt, *Popular Romances,* London: Chatto & Windus, 1903, 118; Bord, *Fairies,* 32.
37 See Brand, *Description of Zetland,* Edinburgh: W. Brown, 1883, 63; J. F. Campbell, *Popular Tales, of the West Highlands.* Edinburgh: Edmonston & Douglas, vol.2, 1860, no.58; Briggs, *Dictionary,* 132.

This Cornish report leads us to the second very frequent type of report from witnesses. It's quite common for people to see fairies *en masse,* apparently drilling like bodies of soldiers. The earliest such report dates from February 1639, when a man at Knaresborough in Yorkshire saw a muster of 'fairies, satyrs and devils' who were training with pikes and muskets in contemporary fashion. Intriguingly, during the Victorian period in a wood outside the same town a witness saw some 'ghosts', dressed in white clothing and armed with swords and commanded by a figure wearing red.[38]

Sightings comparable to that at Knaresborough were common in the succeeding centuries. The Cornish report presumably dates from the 1700s (given the presence of smugglers). Another report from the first half of the same century describes an army seen on Souter Fell in the English Lake District. On Midsummer's Eve, 1735, troops were observed to manoeuvre for nearly an hour on the slopes and precipices of the fell. This display was repeated in 1745, on which occasion five or six people were witness to men, horses and carriages, exercising over a full half mile of land. One of the group who watched this remarkable spectacle climbed up to check the hillside the next day, and found no evidence at all of hoof marks, wheel tracks or any other sign of the passage of large number of soldiers. Given the fairies' habit of foretelling coming events through 'pantomime', it is possible that this vision predicted the Jacobite rebellion of Bonnie Prince Charlie later that year. Additionally, two men saw a fairy army marching with pikes and muskets near to Leicester in 1707.[39]

---

38   Bodleian Tanner MS67, fo.54, Ashton to Tutton, Feb.16th 1639.
39   Gomme, (ed.) *Gentleman's Magazine Library,* 1885, 61.

There were said to be scores or even hundreds of fairy soldiers seen on the Eastern Green at Penzance; very similar examples come from the Isle of Man during the nineteenth century. In one case, a man saw an 'army' dressed in red; in a second, two men met a fairy army on the road at Mull. They were all dressed in red caps and coats, some mounted, some on foot, and they so filled the highway that the men had to climb over a hedge and wait for quite some time for the host to pass. A third experience, dated to about 1830, involved a man later to become a member of the Manx Parliament, the House of Keys. Out one October night on the way to a harvest supper, he and a friend saw a supernatural glow in a field, within which a "great crowd of little beings" dressed in red "moved back and forth amid the circle of light, as they formed into order like troops drilling." Lastly, on Mellor Moor on the Pennines near Blackburn during the mid-eighteenth century, fairies were often said to appear "in military array... their revolutions conforming in every respect to the movement of modern troops."[40]

These figures have uniforms and are frequently armed. The fairies' preparedness for war is underlined in another account. A shepherd at Lochaweside in south west Scotland stumbled across a fairy armoury hidden in a cave. There he found guns and other weapons in chests studded with brass nails. Despite these witnesses, though, others could not believe that the small folk were capable of such martial violence. Questioned about the appearance of the fairies on Islay, one woman in late Victorian times agreed that they might be seen marching to the sound of pipes but, when asked if they carried arms at

---

40 *Yn Lioar Manninagh* III; Roeder, *Manx Folktales*, Isle of Man: Chiollagh Books, 1993, 7; Bord, *Fairies*, 36 & 42; Evans Wentz, 133.

the same time, she denied it: "they had not pith enough – they were but spirits" she replied. Despite this dismissive remark, the facts speak otherwise.[41]

MAKING WEAPONS

For all this warfare to be prosecuted, there have to be fairies capable of producing weaponry. As we shall see later, they have metal working skills, and the faeswho can make a scythe or a plough can forge a sword or a spear just as easily.

That said, the archetypal weapon of the fairy is the arrow, or elf-bolt, and we know rather more about the detail of their manufacture. In early 1662, Isobel Gowdie, who lived at Auldearn, near to Nairn in north-east Scotland, was accused of being a witch. She was examined on these charges on several occasions and gave a full and detailed confession to her inquisitors, which described many of the practices of her coven. Isobel claimed to have visited fairyland (Elfame) and to have witnessed the making of "elf-arrow heidis." Examined on the afternoon of May 3rd, Isobel's account was as follows:

> "the Divell shapes them with his awn hand, and syne deliveris thame to Elf-boyes, who whyttis and dightis [shape and trim] them with a sharp thing like a paking needle… [Isobel saw this done in the 'Elfes-howssis.'] Thes that dightes thaim are little ones, hollow and boss-baked… [hump or hollow backed]."

---

41 Campbell, *Superstitions of the Highlands & Islands.* Glasgow: James MacLehose & Sons, 1900, 95; Campbell, *Popular Tales,* vol.4, 343.

The arrow heads were then supplied to the coven members, who fired them at people by flicking them from their thumbs. The points would kill even if the victims were wearing armour and even though only a glancing blow was achieved. Isobel confessed to the fact that she and the other coven members had killed at least eighteen people with the weapons.

Isobel was interrogated on four separate occasions. On the last, on May 27th, she returned to the subject of manufacturing the weapons. "I haw sein the Elf-Arrowes maid. The Divell dights [dresses] them and the Elf-boye sqhytes them [whet or block them out]." The witches would fly about on straws or bean stalks, shooting at people.[42]

Evidently, we have a craft workshop here, with a modest kind of production line. The process would appear to be that of knapping flints, with the arrow shape initially roughed out from a suitable piece of stone and with the edge then added by careful flaking. This was very obviously an archaic technique in the human world of the mid-seventeenth century, but still actively employed in Faery.

BATTLES

What are these troops exercising for? Direct accounts of fairy fighting are much rarer that the glimpses of them parading. A woman lost in mist saw a pixie battle being fought on the ramparts of Castle-an-Dinas in mid-Cornwall (though, when the fog cleared, though, there was no trace of any fighting). We are told by Mrs Bray that the pixies only gained control

---

42 *Pitcairn's Ancient Criminal Trials in Scotland*, vol.2, part 2, 602–615.

of Devonshire and Dartmoor after a protracted war with the elves. The best example comes from Wales.[43]

> "There is a tradition among the Glamorgan peasantry of a fairy battle fought on the mountain between Merthyr and Aberdare, in which the pigmy combatants were on horseback. There appeared to be two armies, one of which was mounted on milk-white steeds, and the other on horses of jet-black. They rode at each other with the utmost fury and their swords could be seen flashing in the air like so many penknife blades. The army on the white horses won the day, and drove the black-mounted force from the field. The whole scene then disappeared in a light mist."

In a fascinating incident from Greenie, in north-west Orkney, a witness saw a fairy army marching past a well-known fairy knoll. The men were in well-ordered ranks six deep, with guns and swords and under the command of officers. They vanished when they reached a wall. He wasn't alone in seeing this sight, though. Firstly, the dog of the house he was visiting saw the troops pass too, and barked until they had gone; more importantly, he met another person who had also seen the troops marching, but had then seen them fighting. The troops issued from two different knolls, met between them and engaged in dreadful slaughter. After they had struggled for some time, both sides withdrew to their hills and other men emerged to recover the casualties.[44]

---

43 Bray, *Peep on Pixies*, London: Grant and Griffith, 1854, 11; E. Tregarthen, *Pixie Folklore & Legends*, New York: Gramercy Books, 1996, 67–75; Wirt Sikes, *British Goblins*, London: Sampson Low,1880, 107.
44 *Old Lore Miscellany, Orkney and Shetland*, vol.3, 1909, 211.

What is especially interesting about this is the fact that there is also a tale of conflict between the white fairy king and the black at Strath Spey in Scotland. They are said to be locked in perpetual struggle over the white king's wife. This story may give us a hint as to the fairies' motivation for their aggression. For the Spey kings, the prize is possession of a woman; Shakespeare may take us a little nearer the truth with his notion in *A Midsummer Night's Dream* of Oberon and Titania feuding over a changeling boy. It seems very likely that the commonest motive for fairy wars is control of resources – and for the faes, those contested assets are human, whether it is produce they can steal from us or individuals whom they can abduct.[45]

Finally, in one way or another, humans are intimately associated with fairy warfare. For the last example we return to the Isle of Man.

> "A woman walking over Barrule met two fairy armies going to battle, which was to begin on the ringing of a bell; she pulled the bell, and in consequence both armies attacked her, and kept her prisoner for three years, when she escaped."[46]

---

45 Mackenzie, *Scottish Wonder Tales,* London: Blackie & Sons,1917, c.3, 50.
46 *Choice Notes & Queries – Folklore,* 1859, 26.

Faery Society and Faery Work

It is often said that there are two categories of fairy being: the solitary and the 'trooping' or communal. Humans encounter fairies from each group about as frequently, but clearly the 'trooping fairies' are numerically far more numerous. The manner in which fairies choose to live has, of course, profound implications for their needs and their economy.

The solitary beings are the English brownies (and a few pixies), Scottish broonies, some trows on Shetland, various beings of the Highlands, such as the *gruagach, loireag, glaistig* and *uruisg* (or urisk) and the Manx *fynoderee*. All of these tend to live with – or in close proximity to – humans, undertaking domestic chores and the more arduous tasks around a farm or smallholding. The *quid pro quo* for these unstinting and dedicated labours will be an offering or tribute, or a gift, of food – very often milk or some other dairy product, perhaps accompanied by bread.[47] I say offering because, if aggrieved or offended, the fairy can often wreak havoc, undoing all the work done and injuring the very beasts and crops it had previously tended. This exchange is expected, but it must never be thought of as wages. The wrong recompense for the fairy's trouble

---

47   Carmichael, *Carmina Gadelica,* Edinburgh: Oliver & Boyd, vol.2, 1900, 306 & 320.

(clothes instead of food – or the wrong quality of clothes) or the creation of any sense of obligation or subservience to the humans, will drive away the sprite. The extreme touchiness of the different fairies on this matter suggests how anxious they are to preserve their independence. They may be 'domestic' but they are not domesticated; they do not want to be seen to be controlled by a human, nor reliant upon one. It is a curious relationship therefore: prodigious labours can be carried out uninvited and, to all intents and purposes, for free, but all of this is performed at the choosing of the fairy. They are not paid employees, but free agents providing their skills because they choose to do so. Whatever the proper description of this relationship though, these solitary fairies derive food and shelter from the households with which they form their connection. Otherwise, their needs are very simple. As explained, providing clothing is a grave solecism and these beings are usually happy to be naked or to wear only rags.

The communal fairies, in contrast, live in a group. Whether we describe that as the court of a monarch, the following of a chief or leader, a clan, an extended household, or just a family, there will be a (possibly large) number of fairies all resident together. They are to be found living inside hills or in caverns beneath to ground. Whatever the exact subterranean location and whatever the precise arrangement, the economy of that community is going to have to be well organised, so that food and other supplies can be acquired, prepared and distributed.

A highly sophisticated system will be required to produce, in bulk, foodstuffs, drink, clothing, utensils, furnishings and all the other items that fairy aristocracy might desire – jewels, musical instruments, trained horses and hunting dogs. These must be delivered, repaired and replaced.

GETTING THINGS DONE

Most fairies live subject to a clear and probably strict hierarchy – this arises from function but probably involves some sense of rank as well. Some will engage in productive activities; many will lead a life of pure leisure. As we shall see in later chapters, there are crafts and skills exercised by fairies but there also appear to be tasks which they consider to be beneath their dignity. These are the functions that are very often performed for them by humans.

The enslaved or captive human workforce is quite a significant element of fairy society. That humans can be reduced to utter servitude is confirmed by one story from Athol in Perthshire. A widow enquired of the local wise man, Alasdair Callum, what had become of her husband. She was told that he was with the fairies of Slevach Cairn, put to work as a baggage horse with a twisted willow withy in his mouth.[48]

There are several examples of such enforced labour in the folk lore. The workers are abducted by the fairies by three means: by the appearance of death, by the substitution of a changeling or by simple kidnapping. For example, in the Cornish story, *The Fairy House on Selena Moor,* a man meets with his former girlfriend, whom he had thought dead. In fact, she has been abducted to act as a maid for to serve during feasting at the fairy house. Similarly, in the Scottish account of the *Tacksman of Auchriachan,* the farmer or tacksmen meets a woman he believed had died some time before but who is actually serving as cook and housekeeper to a group of demanding fairies. In a story from Badenoch, a man sees a woman spinning and

---

48 Campbell, *Superstitions,* 94.

carding in the fairy hill. She is someone who had died a century ago, so far as her neighbours believed.[49]

In another Scottish account, a girl drives her father's cattle to pasture and passes a fairy knoll. She meets a band of fairies that seize her and carry her inside, where she is set to work. She must bake all the meal stored in the kitchens into bread and, until she has done this, spells will bind her and prevent her returning home. If she completes the task, she will be paid and freed. The situation isn't ideal, but the flour bin doesn't look large, so that it doesn't seem that the task will take her too long. However, it refills every time it's emptied, so that the girl realises she is trapped forever in the fairy hill. Fortunately, another captive is an old woman who was abducted by the fairies in her youth. She pities the girl and tells her how to break the spells. Every time she bakes, the flour she uses on the work surface when she's shaping the dough should be returned to the bin. The effect of this is to stop it refilling. By this ruse, the girl empties the bin. The fairies must reluctantly free her as they had promised, but a terrible curse falls upon the old woman who betrayed them. In another version of this story, the tasks also include spinning a tuft of wool on a distaff; this task is brought to completion on the advice of the other captive by 'spinning the tuft as the sheep bites the hillock': in other words, by drawing the wool in small tufts.[50]

That it is the repetitive and onerous tasks that the fairies do not want to do themselves to which humans are subjected is confirmed by a third story from the Scottish island of Islay. A blacksmith's son, aged fourteen, falls suddenly ill, being taken

---

49 Bottrell, *Traditions & Hearthside Stories*, vol.2, 95; Keightley, *Fairy Mythology*, London: G. Bell, 1850, 390; Campbell, *Popular Tales*, 76.
50 MacDougall & Calder, *Folk Tales & Fairy Lore*, 159; Campbell, *Superstitions*, 67 & 68.

by the fairies and with a changeling left in his place. This impostor is expelled by his father, but he has to go to rescue his son from the knoll. The smith finds him there, working at a forge, and is able to free him. The boy inherits considerable metal working skills from this experience, which is curious given that the account suggests that the hard labour in the heat and dirt of the forge was something that his captors wished to avoid.[51]

CHILD BIRTH AND CHILD REARING

Whilst, as we shall see, the fairies can be talented metal workers or cloth makers, there are some abilities that they seemingly lack. Folklore sometimes tells of fairies granting healing skills to humans, but probably more frequently we hear of fairies needing human medical knowledge – most commonly during childbirth. Midwives are very often paid to attend fairy mothers in labour as there is apparently no accumulated knowledge of obstetrics in Faery. These women are notable for the fact that they are *not* held captive, but are returned to their homes once the baby has been delivered. This may seem surprising, given the discussion previously, and it is a little perplexing to explain. Childbirth, patently, is infrequent and the services of a midwife are not needed daily, weekly or even monthly. Keeping a midwife 'in the hill' would therefore not be economic, as her keep would not be balanced by her utility. At the same time, keeping the midwife favourable and helpful by paying her very generously and

---

51   Campbell, *Popular Tales,* vol.2, 57, no.28.

letting her go home must be calculated to be in the fairies' interests. In one case from the Isle of Skye, for instance, the midwife was detained for eight days in the hill caring for the mother and the new born child (although it seemed only a day to her). When she returned to her home, she was delighted to find that the fairies had cared for her cows during her absence. This kind of gesture would obviously retain her loyalty for when her services were needed again.[52]

The relevance of the occasional necessity (childbirth) contrasted to the daily need for cooking and cleaning probably explains the fairy tendency to abduct nursing mothers. Whilst the fairy infant is suckling and is not wholly dependent upon solid foods, a wet nurse will be required to be present constantly. Accordingly, young women just delivered of babies are often abducted to Faery. It might reasonably be wondered why fairy mothers can't breast-feed their own offspring. There may be physiological reasons we do not know about; it is possibly more likely that the fairy mothers simply think they have better things to do. Why spend time feeding a child when a human skivvy can take care of those physical functions and you can return to the feasting and fun in the hall?[53]

---

52 Askew Roberts, *Bye Gones,* Dec. 24th 1889, 286; McCulloch, 'Folklore of the Isle of Skye,' *Folklore,* vol.32, 1922, 204.
53 Gregor, *Notes on Folklore of the North East of Scotland,* London: Folklore Society, 1881,62.

Faery Gold and Faery Money

"White money, Puck, white fairie money…"[54]

There is much speculation and confusion about the nature of fairy wealth – or the need of fairies for it. Their economy often seems to function without the need for currency at all: rather, they transact all commerce solely on the basis of barter. At the same time, though, it has been alleged that the fairies 'have plenty of money at their command, which they could bestow on people whom they liked.'[55]

Playwright Ben Jonson played upon several notions of the bestowal of fairy wealth in *Eastward Ho!* Impoverished Gertrude wishes fairies still existed, explaining to her maid Sindefy that they could then:

"do miracles and bring ladies money. Sure, if we lay in a cleanly house, they would haunt it, Sin! I'll try. I'll sweep the chamber soon at night, and set a dish of water on the hearth. A fairy may come, and bring a pearl or a diamond. We do

---

54 The Mask at Cole Orton, 1618.
55 see Bottrell, *Traditions and Hearthside Stories,* vol.2 162 – faeries bartering at a market; Evans Wentz, *Fairy Faith,* 142.

not know, Sin. Or there may be a pot of gold hidden o' the backside, if we had tools to dig for it."[56]

The conversation reveals several conceptions about fairy wealth: that it may be bestowed upon those who are seen to be fit and deserving, because their habits please the fairies; or, that it may granted unpredictably, perhaps in the form of buried treasure.

Fairy money can come to humans in far more prosaic ways, nevertheless. For example, it was reported in the 1880s how Evan Thomas of YsguborGerrig, near Llanrwst in Snowdonia, had hired out his cowhouse to the fairies as a shelter from bad weather – a service for which he had, apparently, been very well paid by them.[57]

SOURCES OF FAIRY WEALTH

Where exactly all these coins that are given to favourites come from is an interesting question. We might conclude that the money the fairies leave is actually stolen, lost or perhaps comes from a hidden hoard they have discovered – which may indeed explain the ancient or unknown coins that are sometimes received by way of payment. In the past, this seems to have led to confusion between what was fairy money and what were genuine antiquities – for example, Roman coins found in Herefordshire at Bolitree and Kenchester were taken to be fae coinage by the locals. William Harrison in 1577 described

---

56 Ben Jonson, *Eastward Ho!*, 1605, Act V, scene 1.
57 *North Wales Chronicle & Advertiser,* July 19th 1884, 4– 'City & Country Chit Chat.'

such coins: "Much of their coyne also is to be founde, and some peeces are dayly taken up, which they call borrowe pence, dwarfes money, hegges pence, feirygrootes…"[58]

It has also been alleged that the fairies steal from the rich to assist the poor – like Robin Hood – and there is no denying the evidence that they have a tendency to assist those who are unfortunate and in genuine need.[59]

There are other possible sources of their wealth, though. The fays have been known to enter into contracts with humans – for example, for building work – for which they have agreed payment. Remuneration for services rendered may be in cash – but payment in kind might also be accepted. In around 1855, a Westmorland farmer was walking home one night between Kirkby Lonsdale and Lupton when he found the highway blocked by a 'hedge.' A small man then appeared and offered to help him get through the hedge in return for a pound of the butter he was carrying. The farmer agreed, paid up and was soon on his way again. On the Isle of Man, it's said that the fairies will assist with dairy work in return for a little of the butter or cheese. Somewhat similar is another Manx story concerning a little girl who comes across a fairy market: the stall-holders accept locks of her blonde hair in payment for sweets as they say that it is 'fairy gold.'[60]

---

58 Jones, *Appearance of Evil*, Cardiff: University of Wales Press, 2003, no.70; Anon, *Folklore & Legends*, 1; R. Palmer, *Folklore of Hereford and Worcester*, Hereford: Logaston Press,1992,125; Simpson, *Folklore of the Welsh Border*, London: Harper Collins, 1976, 77; W. Harrison, *Historical Description of the Island of Britain*, vol.II, chapter 17, fo.92.

59 Owen, *Welsh Folklore*, Oswestry: Woodall, Minshall & Co, 1896, 72; Aitken, H. *A Forgotten Heritage – Original Folk Tales of Lowland Scotland*. Scottish Academic Press, 1973, 21.

60 Leney, *Shadowland*, London: Elliott Stock, 1890; Dora Broome, *More Fairy Tales from the Isle of Man*, Douglas: NMP Books, 1970, 12.

Although there are frequent reports of invisible fairies thieving from markets and fairs, they will also engage in normal commercial activities with humans. For example, a man taking a horse to market on the Isle of Man was met by a small man who asked to buy the steed. A bargain was struck after which the buyer mounted his new horse – and promptly sank into the earth. The seller sought the advice of a priest upon the cash he'd received, but was told it was safe to keep it as it had come from a fair deal. A related story is that of Canobie Dick, from the Scottish Borders. Leading a pair of horses over the Eildon Hills, he was approached by an old man in outdated clothes who asked to buy the animals. A bargain was agreed and Dick was paid "in unicorns, bonnet-pieces and other ancient coins." Although it was troublesome disposing of this old currency, Dick began to deal regularly with this buyer – until his faery nature was revealed in dramatic fashion. Buying and selling in the ordinary manner will evidently account for some fairy money (see the chapter on *Fairy Commerce* later).[61]

In Devonshire, it was believed that a penny placed on your table overnight would be taken by the pixies who, in return, would clean the house whilst you slept. It has to be said, though, that examples of paying the fairies for anything (as opposed to offerings and 'protection money') are exceedingly rare and, in the case of domestic brownies who labour devotedly for certain households, the mere suggestion that they might be offered a wage is often sufficient to drive them away forever.[62]

---

61 Waldron, *Isle of Man*, 34; K. Briggs, *Folk Tales and Legends: A Sampler*, 1977, 233.
62 *Reports and Transactions of the Devonshire Association*, vol.8, 1876, 57.

In the Scottish Highlands, at least, fairies will undertake work if they hear a person wish for their task to be completed. They then demand payment for the job done, though the circumstances tend to render this a rather involuntary bargain, frequently with extortionate terms imposed. For example, a man was digging his fields in spring but was forced to stop by the fading light. He wished to himself that the back-breaking job was completed and this idle thought constituted for the fairies a 'night wish' (in Gaelic: *ordachadh-oidche*) which was effectively an invitation to undertake a contract. They complied and by morning all his fields had been dug over ready for the seed to be sown. A fairy had remained behind to agree their remuneration for the work they'd already done, but he only asked for a sheaf of corn for each labourer, a modest request that the farmer was happy to agree to. His crops grew well and he had an excellent harvest with nine stacks of corn gathered. Then the fairies arrived to collect their pay – and there were so many that they stripped the farm of every sheaf. In some versions of this story, the fairy claims 'as much corn as can be carried in a rope on the shoulder.' The farmer agrees to this, because the amount will be modest, but of course the fairy has a magical rope that can encompass the entire crop. Fortunately for the farmer, the rope breaks and his harvest is saved.[63]

A very similar account comes from the Isle of Skye. A man was looking at the crops in his fields and thought to himself that the corn was ready to cut. To the eavesdropping fairies, this was sufficient invitation and overnight they cut it all and

---

63 McPhail, 'Hebrides Folklore,' *Folklore,* vol.11, 1900, 441; C. Robertson, 'Folklore from the West of Ross-shire,' *Transactions of the Gaelic Society of Inverness,* vol.26, 1905, 272.

stacked it in stooks. Then a little man dressed in blue appeared to demand his pay for the work he'd done unbidden. Luckily, all he asked for was a few potatoes and a little pot. This was gladly supplied; but the next day he came again to ask for more – and the day after that, and so on. Eventually the fairies had to be got rid of with a trick – telling them their hill was on fire. A version of this story from Craignish in Argyll has a neighbour bring the bad news, in this case motivated by jealousy over the good fortune of having the fairies do all your work in record time.[64]

Comparable stories are told on Shetland, but there the trows were more proactive in ensuring their remuneration. A man carelessly said to himself that he'd give his best ox to have his corn harvested and, sure enough, within a short time two trows were seen to be reaping in the field. The work was soon done but, when the trows tried to lead off the ox, the man objected and killed one of them with an axe. Where the fairy blood fell, the crops ever afterwards grew red. It is surprising that the retribution was no more severe than this. In another Shetland story, a farmer was engaged in a boundary dispute with his neighbours, whose cattle had strayed into his fields and eaten crops. One night he wished to himself that he had a good ditch and wall around his land, a defence for which he'd give his best cow. The trows were aware of his thoughts and, when he awoke the next morning, he found that the dyke had been constructed – but that his best oxen had been killed by fairy arrows.[65]

---

64 McCulloch, 'Folklore of the Isle of Skye,' *Folklore*, vol.34, 1922, 205; see too Campbell, *Superstitions*, 97.
65 Nicolson, *Shetland Folklore*, 84.

In light of this incident, you might have supposed that this farmer would have been more cautious in what he wished for. This was not so. Freed from the trespasses of strangers' cattle, he had an excellent crop in his fields and wished to himself that his grain was harvested (and for the saving of this labour, he'd again give his best cow). The trows once again overheard and got his crops in during the night – but another cow was left dead.[66]

From these accounts it appears that the fairies normally prefer to be paid in kind rather than in cash. Other instances confirm this impression. On a farm at Craiginnan in Clackmannanshire, the fairies helped with the hay harvest, in return for a few of the best fleeces at sheep shearing time. Of course, when the farmer's son took over the holding and begrudged them their pay, they undid all their work in the fields in revenge. At Largs, in Ayrshire, fairies helped on a farm in return for shoes and stockings. On Bute, it was said that the fairies would help get in the stooks at harvest in return for bread bannocks and milk. On Exmoor, bread, milk and water was sufficient recompense for pixies, who would enter homes at night, finish off the brewing and clean the dwelling. A meal left out in the field would be accepted in return for reaping the corn. On the Channel Island of Jersey, the belief was that, if a piece of cake were left out at bed time by a servant, the fairies would undertake all her unfinished chores overnight – as well as doing a portion of the following day's tasks as well. For the same inducement, these same fairies would also complete needlework; all the housewife needed to do was to provide needle, thread and cake. This compares to the Staffordshire habit of rewarding the fairies for finding lost items with cake

---

66 J. Haldane-Burgess, 'Some Shetland Folklore', *Scottish Review*, vol.25, 1895, 98 & 100.

– and the practice in the same county of leaving cake as a gift for fairies who came into people's homes at night.[67]

It seems too that the fairies may sometimes just work for the pleasure of working – and will help out humans uninvited. For example, fairies at Pennygowan on Mull would happily undertake spinning and weaving work overnight, without charge, if the materials were left outside their hill along with a sample of what was wanted, or a spoken request. One man abused this, however, leaving a short length of wood and asking for a ship's mast to be manufactured. The fairies laboured all night on this, cursing all the while at what had been asked of them. They completed the task – but never undertook another after that. Abuse of fairy generosity that leads to its cessation is a persistent theme in our folklore.[68]

Even so, these helpful faes can still overstay their welcome and become a nuisance, demanding more and more work after the original task they volunteered to undertake has been completed. Their enthusiasm for performing a task together may be judged by the fact that several work-songs that have been recorded – for example, fairies on Skye sang:

> "Let me comb, card, tease, spin,
>   Get a weaving loom quick,
>   Water for fulling on the fire,
>   Work, work, work."[69]

67　Campbell, *Superstitions*, 77; 'Collecteanea,' *Folklore,* vol.25, 1913, 245; Hewison, *The Isle of Bute in Olden Time,* Edinburgh and London, William Blackwood and Sons, 1893, vol.2, 266; Snell, *Book of Exmoor,* London: Methuen, 1903, 254–256; *Folklore,* vol.25, 1914, 245; Burne, 'Staffordshire folk and their lore,' *Folklore,* vol.7, 1896, 398; Cope, *Memorials of Old Staffordshire,* London: George, Allen & Unwin, 1909, 89.

68　Campbell, *Superstitions,* 59.

69　Campbell, *Superstitions,* 75.

Fairy folk have also been known to make 'profit sharing' agreements with humans – usually miners. In one highly exceptional report, Dartmoor pixies were said to receive coins as offerings from cottagers to persuade them to tidy the houses. This runs directly counter to the usual arrangement where a coin is left in recognition of a home being left clean and tidy for when the fairies visit at night.[70]

As shall be described later, the fairies are known to indulge in commercial enterprise, manufacturing goods and growing food which might be sold for profit, so much of their reported wealth may have been obtained by honest labour and clever entrepreneurship. There are suggestions though of less lawful sources of income. In one Cornish story, a woman out one moonlit night picking 'pisky-stools' (mushrooms) on the cliffs near Padstow meets the piskies coming up from the beach with burdens on their backs. They tell her that these bags are in fact their beds. Although the evening was one on which we might anticipate finding the fairies dancing, we must suspect that the moonlight on this occasion illuminated smuggling instead.

A last – and especially surprising – source of fairy money is moneylending. This hardly seems like a conventional fairy activity, but one early seventeenth century text tells us this about 'the trickes of women fayries':

> "We often use to dwell in some great hill, and from thence we
> doe lend money to any poore man or woman that hath need;
> but if they bring it not againe at the day appointed, we doe

---

70 Deane & Shaw, *Folklore of Cornwall*, Stroud: The History Press, 2009, 69; Crossing, *Tales of Dartmoor Pixies,* Newcastle upon Tyne: F. Graham,1890,c.3.

not only punish them with pinching, but also in their goods, so that they never thrive till they have payd us."

We know the risks of borrowing from human banks, but supernatural lenders are yet more dangerous creditors to have.[71]

PAYMENTS TO HUMANS

"These fayery favours/ Are lost when not conceal'd."[72]

The fairies have coin, it appears, because they have a variety of dealings with humans and because they know that – to us – hard cash is important. For this reason, they acquire money in order to pay people for services rendered to them or in order to reward those whom they choose to favour.[73] They may be very generous in these cases, for example giving a life time's supply of gold or a purse that never empties.[74]

The fairies are aware of humans' greatest weakness, our greed for gold. They know that, for gold, we may do almost anything and that we may act recklessly to gain it, not thinking of our safety. For instance, a Manx girl walking over a bridge on the island was offered a farthing by three little men. Wisely she refused, knowing that she'd have been carried off if she

---

71 *Robin Goodfellow: His Mad Prankes and Merry Jests,* 1628.

72 J. Dryden, *The Spanish Fryar,* Act II, scene 2, 21.

73 Evans Wentz, *Fairy Faith,* 156; Sternberg, *Dialect and Folklore,* London: J. R. Smith, 1851, 137; Bowker, *Goblin Tales,* London: Swan Sonnenschein, 1878, 'The enchanted fisherman.'

74 Jenkyn Thomas, *Welsh Fairy Book,* New York: F. A. Stokes, 1908, 'Lowri Dafydd;' Marwick *The Folklore of Orkney,* Edinburgh: Birlinn Ltd, 2011, 34.

accepted it. Temptation – and even an element of selling her soul – were evidently involved here.[75]

Even where the money received from the fairies comes as a regular supply of low value coins, over time these can accumulate to a substantial sum. John Aubrey wrote about a Hereford woman who saved up the threepenny bits she regularly found until she had accrued enough to buy a small silver cup or bowl worth as much as £3 (at one coin a week, this would have taken over a year and a half). Katharine Briggs observed that some fairies were more generous than others: while some received sixpences, the tylwyth teg distributed the greatest largesse, leaving their favourites florins and half-crowns – that is, two shillings or 2/6.[76]

It may have been noted that, in many cases, the fairy money is received anonymously; the recipient never sees the giver. Situations where payment is being made for a service rendered may be exceptions – as with pipers and fiddlers taken into the Faery to entertain a gathering or dance. Another exception is Welsh wise man Harry Lloyd who, during the 1540s, was prosecuted before Caernarfon quarter sessions for fortune telling, familiarity with wicked spirits and for cheating the King's subjects. He had met with friendly fairies on Tuesday and Thursday nights and been given gold by them.[77]

In contrast to these cases, there are plenty where money received from the fairies does not turn out to be all that it seemed. Payments or gifts may vanish after they've been received or may transpire later to be shells, withered leaves,

---

75 *Choice Notes & Queries – Folklore,* 1859, 26.

76 Aubrey, *Remains of Gentilisme,* 29 & 125; Briggs, 'The Fairy Economy,' *Folklore* 70, 534.

77 G. Jones, 'Y Tylwyth Teg,' *Llen Cymru,* vol.8, 1965, 96–9.

leather, dead flowers, paper or horse dung. John Locke prudently warned in 1690 that borrowed wealth was "like Fairy money... [it] will be but Leaves and Dust when it comes to use."[78]

Sometimes there's a reason for the disappearance or change in the money: the recipient has betrayed fairy confidences or has been rude or ungrateful;[79] sometimes the transformation doesn't appear to be deserved and the fairies just seem to be mean. For example, an Arran midwife attended a birth in a fairy knoll. Once the child was safely delivered (as is usually the way in these cases), she was asked to anoint its eyes with special ointment. Accidentally touching her own eye, she found she could see through the fairy glamour – which included realising that the payment she had received for her services was not gold, but animal droppings.[80] The opposite transformation may take place as well, though. Change given by the fairies as leaves or pebbles may turn out to be gold.[81]

In connection with the last paragraph, it's worth observing that identical transformations might occur to goods given to humans as well. For instance, a man called Robin Oig was hunting in Glenmore one day when he met a party of fairies marching with music. He claimed a fine set of bag pipes with silver, jewelled chanter and drones by the time-honoured trick of throwing his bonnet and crying out "What's mine is

78 Askew Roberts, *Bye Gones*, May 15th 1895, 88; J. Locke, *An Essay on Human Understanding*, 1690, vol.I, chapter 4, 36.
79 Owen, *Welsh Folklore*, 81 & 82; Jenkyn Thomas, *Welsh Fairy Book*, 'Dick the Fiddler' & 'The Harper's Gratuity.'
80 Owen, *Welsh Folklore*, 84 & 90; Jenkyn Thomas, *Welsh Fairy Book*, 'Guto Bach;' MacKenzie, *Book of Arran*, Arran: Kilbrannan Publishing, 1914, 263.
81 F. Mathews, *Tales of the Blackdown Borderland*, Taunton: Somerset Folk Press,1923, 57

yours and what's yours is mine." The fairies had to relinquish the pipes to him, but when he got home, he discovered what he had obtained was a puff ball mushroom with some broken spikes of grass stuck in it. Stories like these can all be read as tales about the fairies using glamour to deceive greedy humans, but they also suggest that they have a very effective means of stopping any flow of currency or goods out of Faery. They can gain from us – at no expense.[82]

As has already been suggested, receipt of fairy money can be conditional upon discretion – hence widespread popular sayings along the lines that something's "like Fayries Treasur's vanished if reveal'd."[83] Almost always, as soon as the source of unexplained wealth is confessed, it is lost forever and cannot be regained. This is a consistent and very well-known folklore theme: for example, in Beaumont and Fletcher's play *The Honest Man's Fortune*, a character warns, "For when they talk once, 'tis like fairy money,/ They get no more..."

Fairy benevolence can be disclosed, and forfeit, in two different ways. Firstly, the beneficiary may boast or become careless. Tomas Morris, of Tyn-y-Pant in Montgomeryshire, one night came across the fairies dancing in a circle. They promised that he would find gold every night if he joined their dance. He did so, having been enjoined to the strictest secrecy. Of course, in time he talked about his good fortune to others and, inevitably, the next time he went to look for coins, he found only cockle shells. In the most serious cases, the person who betrays the fairies' confidence might fall ill or die. A man of Evershot, Dorset, had for a long time been very

---

82 W. Forsyth, *The Shadow of Cairngorm*, Inverness: The Northern Counties Publishing Company, Ltd., 1900, 186.

83 W. Barksted, *Mirrha*, sig.C5.

poor but suddenly started to find a shilling under his door every morning. He saved the money and in time was able to buy some sheep, then some pigs, so that gradually he became rich. His neighbours marvelled at his wealth and, at last, he confessed how his prosperity had begun. He was instantly struck lame and became bed-ridden, remaining that way for many months.[84]

Secondly, the secret of the fairy gifts may be revealed unwillingly, usually because a child or servant is threatened with a sanction or a beating on suspicion that they have been stealing the coins. This happened to a dairy maid on a Welsh farm, who feared dismissal for dishonesty, and to a boy on Anglesey, whose father forced him to own up. Even though these disclosures are involuntary, the fairy coins will cease to appear.[85]

A story along these lines also gives us an additional perspective into the nature of fairy money itself. A Norfolk ploughman one day found a brand-new silver shilling at the end of the furrow he had been ploughing. The next day he found two; the day after that, four – and so on. His problem in the village where he lived was two-fold – he had to account for his new found and exponentially increasing wealth *and* he had to explain why all this money seemed to be freshly minted. Local traders began to refuse to accept his cash, fearing that he was coining his own false currency and his employer dismissed

---

84 Marwick *The Folklore of Orkney* 34; Beaumont & Fletcher, Act 5, scene 1; E. Owen, 'Folklore Superstitions, Part 4,' *Collections Historical and Archaeological regarding Montgomeryshire*, vol.18, 1885, 143; *Y Cymmrodor*, vol.9, 1886, 384; *Archaeologia Cambrensis*, vol.3, 1886, 72; R. Baxter, *The Certainty of the World of Spirits*, London: Parkhurst & Salisbury, 1691,46.

85 Cobb, 'Anglesey Folklore from near Holyhead,' *Y Cymmrodor*, vol.7, 1886, 197; *Wrexham & Denbighshire Advertiser*, March 9th 1878, 9.

him. Finally, he had to admit to his wife where it was coming from, knowing too that no more would then come.[86]

Very similar is the Manx story of the *Fisherman and the Ben-Varrey*. A poor fisherman sees a *ben-varrey* (a mermaid) in a dream and she advises him to dig near his house. He does so and finds a buried chest, "full of gold pieces of money, queer old coins with strange markings." He stops work, thinking he has become wealthy for the rest of his life, but the money turns out to be worthless to him, as everyone in the local town is suspicious and refuses to take the gold. Fairy money can be a curse as well as a favour then – and there is a least a hint in the Norfolk tale that the fairies themselves may be coiners.[87]

A final intriguing twist upon this theme comes from a Scottish folktale told about a midwife taken to attend the fairy queen. The boy who fetches her is a human enslaved under an enchantment for twenty-one years; he is able to give her various warnings how to behave when she is in Faery. He particularly tells her not to accept payment in either gold or silver from the faes and to throw away any gifts they may give her. She obeys his instructions, casting away the presents made to her after she has left the fairy hill. The items explode into flames – and would have burned her home down had she kept them.[88]

It seems that fairy gold need not come directly from the faes themselves. From April 1623 we have the fascinating record of the interrogation of witch suspect Margaret Hormscleuch in Perth. Amongst her alleged offences (which were mainly healing

---

86 Emerson, 'The ploughman and the Fairies,' *Folklore,* vol.7, 1896, 301.
87 Dora Broome, *Fairy Tales from the Isle of Man,* Douglas: NMP Books, 1968, 115; contrast to this her story of 'The Merman's Coat' in *More Fairy Tales from the Isle of Man,* 1970, 1, in which the gold paid by the merman for his coat enriches a whole village.
88 MacDougall & Calder, *Folk Tales and Fairy Lore,* 271.

sick cattle and people) she was asked "if she gave 'fairy pennies' – that is, some pennies to cause men to thrive and become rich…" Margaret replied to this that she had indeed given some, but she couldn't recall to whom, nor could she remember who had given her these coins in the first place. Margaret was clearly trying to avoid incriminating others, or further incriminating herself, but the belief that fairy money brought good fortune over and above its intrinsic value is notable.[89]

It need hardly be said that, whilst the faeries may share their wealth with those they choose, they are otherwise jealous of it. A story from Polperro, on the Cornish south coast, recounts how a fisherman discovered pixies on the beach one night, counting out their money and sharing it between themselves. He slipped his hat into the ring and got a few coins but, inevitably, when he tried to make off with his gold, he was chased furiously all the way home.[90]

BURIED TREASURE

"And some found heapes of gold,
Long hid in hollow ground."[91]

Faery has long had a traditional connection with buried treasure. Today, perhaps the best-known example is Irish leprechauns, of whom it's said that catching one will lead you to his pot of gold. The subject is far more complex and interesting than this and there is a wealth of British examples

89   T. H. Marshall, *The History of Perth*, Perth: J. Fisher, 1849, 355.
90   Couch, *History of Polperro*, Truro: W. Lake, 1871, 137.
91   From Thomas Churchyard, *A Handful of Gladsome Verses*, 1593.

to illustrate it – for example, in Snowdonia fairy treasure is said to be concealed beneath the *Moel Eilio* mountain and, in fact, so consistently is buried gold connected to the tylwyth teg that the phrase *arian daear* (earth money) has entered the Welsh language.[92]

An indication of how firmly people once believed in the fairies' close association with treasure comes from Penwith in the far west of Cornwall. In 1906 it was widely reported that a Mr Varke, of Goldsithney just outside Marazion, was excavating for buried riches. His grandmother, some half century before, had lived in a cottage at Lower Bodilly, near Wendron, and had been there visited by two pixies, who told her that a vast treasure lay buried beneath her home. Her two sons duly dug up the floor and removed soil to a depth of several fathoms, but found nothing. Forty years on from this, the cottage had been demolished and the grandson decided to renew the search. At the time that the story appeared in the press, he had dug to a depth of twenty-four feet and had a windlass and water pumps set up to help as the shaft got deeper. We don't learn what the outcome was, but Mr Varke may have wished to reflect upon the experience of two men at Le Catillon on Guernsey. In 1829 they started to excavate around a large stone said to be impressed with footprints, marking it as a place beneath which fairy gold was buried. The pair shifted earth all morning and then paused for lunch. When they returned to their task in the afternoon, all the soil that had been removed was back in place; wisely, they could take a hint and they gave up.[93]

---

92 Evans Wentz, *Fairy Faith*, 71 & 82; *Evening Express,* Nov.15th 1899, 2 – 'By the Way;' *North Wales Chronicle*, Dec.12th 1890, 7.

93 *Cardiff Times,* August 25th 1908, 2– 'Treasure Hunt in Cornwall; Pixies and Hidden Riches;' E. MacCulloch, *Guernsey Folklore*, 153.

There are many aspects to the subject of buried treasure, but the starting point must be the fact that fairies hoard, or at least know of the whereabouts, of gold. It is said, for example, that fairy gold is stored at Cadbury Camp in Dorset and also at Dolebury where, to make matters worse, the fairies' magic makes it sink deeper into the ground should anyone come digging in search of it. Thomas Nashe believed instead that the gold was continually moved about underground, so that none could find it. Another writer, Thomas Heywood, was uncertain whether the booty was hidden from us because of the elves' avarice, because God had forbidden it, knowing men's avarice, or because it was all, in fact, merely illusory. As we proceed with this section, you might indeed be inclined to see it all as a fairy deception sent to taunt us.[94]

As with fairy money, the source of this bullion is uncertain. It may have been buried by humans in the past or it may have been collected by the fays. Mermaids are known to gather coins, pearls and bullion from sunken ships. There is even a suggestion that the faes may create it through alchemy. In Cornwall it was believed that lead left out on an ant's nest would be transmuted by the pixies into silver at the New Moon.[95]

I've already mentioned how the fays may actively prevent our finding their wealth. Sometimes they are more aggressive in defence of their hoards. At Craufurdland Bridge, near Kilmarnock, a brownie protected the pot of gold concealed in the pool beneath the crossing and successfully defeated an

94 Tongue, *Somerset Folklore*, London: Folklore Society, 1965, 111; Palmer, *Folklore of Somerset*, London: Harper Collins, 1976, 26; Nashe, *Pierce Pennilesse*, 1592; Heywood, *Hierarchie of Blessed Angels*, 570.
95 Courtney, *Cornish Feasts*, Penzance: Beare & Son, 1890, 125.

attempt to dam and drain the pool by playing a trick on the prospector – he raised the alarm for fire at the man's home and, whilst the men were absent, pulled down the dam. At Abernethy near Perth, the buried gold of a Pictish king was guarded by a dwarf who fiercely assailed any man who came digging. The threat of imminent violence also protected gold concealed at Trencrom Hillfort in West Penwith in Cornwall: a man digging there noticed the sky darkening and, when he looked up, realised that a horde of spriggans was advancing upon him at speed, growing in size as they rapidly approached. He wisely fled home, where he had to take to his bed for several weeks to recover.[96]

In Fife, in Scotland, a pot of fairy gold is reported to be buried in Carden Glen. However, only two brothers will ever be able to find it – and their treasure is cursed. Once the gold has been uncovered, the brothers will quarrel and fight over it and one will die. James Wilkie, who published this story, added the following warning verse:

> "All the gold the fairies have is the gold of the summer sheaf,
> And all the gold the fairies give, it fades with the fading leaf."[97]

A curiously contradictory story from Pembrokeshire has supernatural forces both revealing and defending buried bullion. During the 1820s, a man was troubled by spirits at night. He sought the advice of a local wise woman who recommended that he get up and follow the apparitions in

---

96 Spence, *Fairy Tradition in Britain*, London: Rider & Co, 1948, 38 & 219; Bottrell, *Hearthside Stories*, vol.2, 245; see too Bowker, *Goblin Tales*, 104.

97 J. Wilkie, *Bygone Fife, North of the Lomonds*, Edinburgh & London: William Blackwood & Sons, 1938, 15.

his bedroom. He did this, and followed the spirit to a hedge where it beckoned to him to dig. When he scraped the earth away, he found a valuable silver inkstand buried inside a clay pot. Naturally, he took this home, but as he went, two tiny hobgoblins pelted him with three cornered stones.[98]

Given that the fairies are in possession of great wealth, and given the instinctive greed of many humans, it is inevitable that many have turned their minds to discovering ways to convey this wealth out of the control of its original possessors. Here the interaction between Faery and mortals becomes even more complicated and fraught.[99]

Sometimes it proves possible to extort money from the fairies. In Cornwall, it was believed that a large quantity of gold was concealed around the ancient stone monuments of the county and that, if you could only capture a pisky, spriggan or knocker, it could be forced to disclose the whereabouts of the riches. Of course, the supernatural being would know too that the human captor would become distracted as soon as precious metals got involved, creating opportunities to escape. Nevertheless, the canny and determined individual might make himself rich very easily this way, as was the case for a man from Rockingham in Northamptonshire, who caught an elf called the 'redman' and constrained it to reveal its cache of gold.[100]

Force doesn't have to be involved. The fairies may willingly lead favoured individuals to the buried treasure – or may just place it in front of them. For example, a Scottish pedlar in Ayrshire was approached by a fairy woman who wanted to

98 *Cardiff Times*, June 11th 1904, 1– 'Pembrokeshire Folklore.'
99 Chapman, Jonson & Marston, *Eastward Hoe*, IV, 1.
100 Bottrell, vol.1, 74; Hill *Folklore of Northamptonshire*, Stroud: The History Press, 2005,152.

buy one of the bowls he was selling. He refused to sell for some reason and, a short while later, dropped his basket. Only the bowl the woman had asked for was broken, whilst, later that same day, he discovered a hidden treasure that more than compensated for the price of the lost vessel. The fairies don't always need a reason to bestow good fortune, though: a man came across the fairies dancing on the beach at Puckaster Cove on the Isle of Wight. He joined the dance but, after a while, needed to sit and rest. He sat on something like a puffball mushroom which burst, showering gold dust everywhere. The faeries gave him some of this before he parted from their company.[101]

Rather than giving the humans the wealth, the fairies might alternatively lead them to where it was concealed. This might be done by various means: for instance, at Bury Castle near Clun in Shropshire, it's said that the fairies have left a thin gold wire to guide treasure seekers to the pot of gold they buried. In *The Secret Commonwealth*, the Reverend Robert Kirk described how two women one night in 1676 received a vision that treasure was buried in a nearby fairy hill. Firstly, they each saw the hoard, then they heard a voice. Going to the spot, they met and together dug up a vessel containing ancient coins, which they shared between them. This vision was sent to the women at a time of famine, so that they might buy food for the people. In a similar story from Wales, a boy called Guto Bach was guided by the fairies to look under a rock where he found gold and

---

101 Spence, *Fairy Tradition*, 220; and see Ben Jonson, *The Silent Woman*, V, 1– gifts of jewels.

silver concealed, after his parents had lost their money in a shipwreck.[102]

Lastly, the fairies might bestow a magical power to detect buried treasure upon an individual. This gift was claimed in 1499 by Marion Clerk of Great Ashfield in Suffolk. She was prosecuted before a Church court in Norwich for claiming that the faeries helped her locate buried treasure by providing her with a rod of holly for this purpose. She had charged people 2/– each for her treasure seeking service.

Access to free riches sounds enticing, but a condition might be attached. For instance, at Bamburgh in Northumberland there is a rock where people may find caches of coins, placed there by the fairies. This wealth cannot simply be pocketed, however: the finder is obliged to leave a silver coin of their own at the spot in order to ensure that the treasure will be found again.[103]

Sometimes, though, despite the visions and the guidance, the prospectors fail to find the hidden gold. What's not clear is whether this was just down to their poor excavating or because the fairies never meant them to have it in the first place. The folklore on this is contradictory. An Aberdeen man called Walter Rolandson had been visited by a fairy in the form of a child twice a year for 27 years or so. In 1601, it came to him in bed, sitting on his chest and calling his name. He was told to go to a certain place and dig, for he would find gold, silver and other valuable property. Ronaldson did so, but found nothing. Despite his failure, he remained

---

102 Morrison, *Manx Fairy Tales,* London: D. Nutt,1911, 'Themselves;' Simpson, W*elsh Borders,* 28; Kirk, c.10; Jenkyn Thomas, *Welsh Fairy Book,* 'Guto Bach.'
103 Spence, *Fairy Tradition,* 218.

convinced the riches were present: "there is gold there, gif it were weel sought" he told a church court.[104]

Just a few years later, a woman called Susan Swapper, living in Rye is Sussex, was visited by four fairies at night. First, they told her to dig in a friend's garden within the town. She found nothing but was "troubled by treasure" until the fairies told her to dig for a pot of gold buried in a field outside the town. She did as she was instructed, but again failed to find any hoard; nonetheless, she met the fairy queen who told her that, if she was prepared to make submission to her, she would never want for money for the rest of her life. A similar tale of riches withheld but some compensation offered comes from lowland Scotland. A girl was sat by a well spinning wool on a distaff when she looked into the depths of the water and saw a pot of gold beneath the surface. Marking the spot with her spindle, she ran to tell her father. He suspected it was glamour intended to trap and drown her and, sure enough, when they returned to the place, the moor was covered in distaffs. Nonetheless, twelve men in green appeared and returned her original spindle with its wool all spun.[105]

On other occasions, the visions of hidden treasures are much more plainly a fairy tease. In late 1662, the London household of the Mompessons were troubled by noises, such as drummings and the sound of money chinking. The family were advised that this was the fairies indicating to them that coins were hidden somewhere about the house. On the Isle of Man, the fairies whispered to a man drowsing on his sofa

---

104 Dalyell, *Darker Superstitions*, Edinburgh: Waugh & Innes, 1834, 531.
105 Aitken, *Forgotten Heritage*, 18.

about hidden gold; in shock he fell onto the floor, was ill for six months and was lamed for the remainder of his life.[106]

Worse still are the cases where the fairies taunted the humans with a sight of the gold – and then withheld it from them. This is demonstrated in two Welsh reports. In one case, a girl walking on the mountains near her home came upon a solid golden chair. It was too heavy for her to have any hope of carrying it home, so she tried to mark the spot so that she could find her way back by using the thread from the spindle she had with her. She tied one end to a stone by the chair and unravelled the ball as she made her way home; there was only just enough to lead her back to her parents' cottage. The next morning, of course, the thread was gone and the prize was lost forever. In a comparable story, a man discovered a cache of gold concealed in a cave. His only way of being able to retrace his route was to cut chips from his walking staff to mark the way back to his farm. The next morning, these too had disappeared.[107]

Lastly, and as ever, discretion about the source of riches is enjoined. If the finder talks too freely, all will be lost: as Thomas Heyrick wrote in *The New Atlantis*, "Like fairy treasure, if disclosed, is gone." A practical demonstration of this comes from Montgomeryshire in South Wales. A weaver called David was crossing the mountain near Llugry one day when he was approached by two fairies who asked him to accompany them to see a hidden chest of gold. He went with them, of course, and marked the spot with his walking stick before going home to share the good news with his wife. He

---

106 J. Glanvill, *Saducismus Triumphatus*, 1668, vol.II, 95; *Choice Notes & Queries – Folklore*, 26.
107 Owen, *Welsh Folklore*, 72.

warned her to keep the find a secret, but she felt impelled to share their good news with a neighbour – who went and took the gold first.[108]

These experiences take us back to one of our earlier points and very much confirm the suspicion that fairy gold is, very much of the time, a matter of illusion and temptation, a mockery of human cupidity that is never meant to be satisfied.[109]

108 Heyrick, 1687, 15; E. Owen, 'Folklore Superstitions, Part 4,' *Collections Historical and Archaeological Regarding Montgomeryshire,* vol.18, 1885, 141.
109 George Chapman, *A Humorous Day's Mirth.*

Farming Fairies

Our conventional view of the faeries is of a people of wild or wooded places whose life is one long round of leisure and pleasure – dancing, feasting and the like. At the same time, we don't tend to imagine them having any concerns with bread-winning or the means of production – indeed, a strong antipathy for such occupations has often been imagined. There's a widespread rhyme in Scotland to the effect that:

> "Where the scythe cuts and the sock (plough) rives,
> Hae done wi' fairies and bee-bykes."

This gloomy view is mistaken. To begin with, a moment's reflection will remind us of the farm labouring brownies, for example, and when the sources are examined, consistent fairy links to agriculture are revealed – as are their interests in manufacture, mining, cloth-making, building and the like. The fairy economy is as complex as our own.

Fairies are often believed to rely solely upon stolen dairy products and corn, preying on them "as do Crowes and Mice" as Robert Kirk memorably put it. These thefts might be more or less blatant. Glamour could be deployed to cover up – and even restore – their depredations, as in the cases where the fairies were said to refill vats and grain bins and to save the hide and bones of slaughtered cows and then use these to resurrect the beast, whole and healthy, so that the farmer would never know what had happened.[110]

The other common method of stealing human crops is to take their vital substance, their 'benefit', whilst leaving the physical produce behind. In one story from Skye, the fairies came to extract the *toradh* from a farmer's field of grain, but were chased away by his dog. As they left, they loudly complained that the hound would have been faster still had he been fed on thin porridge. The farmer overheard (as was intended) and duly gave the dog the recommended meal. As the fairies foresaw, the dog ate too much of the watery dish and was then too full to run after them, so that their theft could be completed unimpeded.[111]

In fact, despite these stories, the fairies have been observed actively involving themselves in all aspects of farming. As I've discussed before, they have their own goats and other livestock. These are distinctly different from humans' beasts, although the faeries may also acquire ours, sometimes by surreptitiously luring them away and sometimes slightly more honestly. In the book, *A Pleasant Treatise of Witches*, the author recounted a story he had heard of a pregnant sow that was fed daily by the fairies with bread and milk. When farrowing time came, they clearly felt they were entitled to the fruit of their investment in the pig: they took all the piglets but left their value in silver behind. This wasn't theft, but it wasn't a normal purchase either and, as such, is the epitome

---

110 *Secret Commonwealth* c.1; Scot, *The Discoverie of Witchcraft*, Book III, c.2; Coxhead, *Devon Traditions*, Exmouth: Deiderfield & Sons,1959, 51.
111 Campbell, *Superstitions*, 56.

of Faery. It's non-consensual for the human farmer, it asserts a presumed right over our goods and, yet, there is something in exchange.[112]

On the whole, our evidence suggests that fairy livestock is of an extremely high quality and is highly desirable to human farmers. There are numerous stories of people profiting from having fairy cattle in their herds, or bearing the offspring of fairy sires; one of the best known is that of the fairy cow of Llyn Barfog, which was known as the *Fuwch Gyfeiliorn* (the stray cow). This beast was one of the *gwarddeg y llyn,* the fairy lake cattle, which a man managed to capture and pen. It was famed in his locality for its milk, cheese, butter and calves. Eventually, after many years of productivity, the man judged it was time to fatten the beast for slaughter. The fairies discovered his intention, and called the heifer home – with all the generations of her daughters – ruining the farmer.[113]

We know already from the reports of visitors that the fays have their own fields and orchards in fairyland underground, but most witnesses of course don't see them there. The Reverend Kirk believed that our landscape here and there showed the marks of the fairies' cultivation from a time that preceded the country's occupation by humankind:

"Albeit, when severall Countreys were uninhabited by us,
these had their easy Tillage above Ground, as we now.
The Print of those Furrows do yet remain to be seen on

---

112 Anon, *A Pleasant Treatise of Witches,* London: C. Wilkinson, Thomas Archer and Thomas Burrell. 1673.
113 *Cardigan Bay Visitor,* Sept. 7th 1892, 4.

the Shoulders of very high Hills, which was done when champayn Ground was Wood and Forrest."[114]

As mentioned earlier, too, some land in our world seems to be set aside for the fairies to use, the intention being either to leave an area undisturbed for the fays – or it may have been an allowance for them to continue to farm.[115]

By and large, though, the fairies have retreated to their subterranean realms which means that, usually, the fays are only to be encountered participating in human farming activities. In fact, they have shown an interest in our pastoral and dairy production, in fruit growing, in horticulture and in the cultivation of grain crops.

FAIRIES AND FERTILITY

In East Anglia, the local fairies are variously called the Yarthkins, the Tiddy Ones, the Strangers or the Greencoaties. As the first name plainly shows, they are rooted in the local soil: 'yarthkin' derives from 'earthkin' and denotes a small spirit born from the land. According to one witness interviewed by Mrs Balfour in the Fens, the diminutive beings are so-called because "tha doolt i' th' mools" ('they dwelt in the soft earth or mould'). The Strangers act as fertility spirits, helping the growth and ripening of plant life. According to Mrs Balfour's late nineteenth century account, in the spring they pinch the

---

114 Kirk, *The Secret Commonwealth*, c.2; see too John McArthur, *The Antiquities of Arran*, 69: ancient plough marks seen at Tor Castle are called 'elf-furrows.'
115 Palmer, *Gloucestershire*, 145.

tree and flower buds to make them open and tug worms out of the earth; they help flowers bloom and green things and then at harvest they make corn and fruits ripen. Without their attention, the plants would shrivel, harvest would fail and people would go hungry. In recognition of this, the Strangers receive tribute or offerings from the local people – the first of any flowers, fruits or vegetables and the first taste of any meal or drink. If neglected, these beings may be vindictive, affecting yields, making livestock sick and even causing children to pine away.[116]

Fertility is, it would seem, a commodity or benefit that the fairies may dispense – or withhold – at their whim. An account from South Devon underlines this starkly. A farmer living near Exmouth was on good terms with the pixies and they ensured that his farm prospered. In recognition of their aid, he provided them with an annual feast, laying out food and drink in his farmhouse and ensuring that they were undisturbed and unobserved whilst they enjoyed it. Eventually, the man died and his sons took over the farm. They continued his traditions, but appointed a new farmhand who did not respect them so much. He was determined to spy on the pixies' yearly banquet, but his presence was quickly detected and they vanished. From that day forth, the prosperity of the farm vanished too. The milk and cream soured, the butter would never churn and cheeses never set, the apples failed, cattle dropped and the crops were blighted.[117]

There is uncertainty about the exact nature of the fairies' connection to plant growth and our reliance upon them for good harvests. One theory about their origins popular with

---

116 See Balfour in *Folklore* vol.2 1891.
117 *Truman's Exeter Flying Post*, August 18th 1869, 6– 'Devonshire Pixies.'

folklorists is that our modern fairies represent the minor fertility gods of Roman times and earlier.[118] Certainly, as the Yarthkins show, they can play a key role in fertility. Examining the British records, you soon discover that there are plentiful indications that the fairies are intricately associated with the weather and plant growth and with the fertility of not just farm livestock but of people too. They are, in general therefore, symbols of natural life in all its forms.

The intimate links between the balance within Faery and the health of the human world is brought out in Shakespeare's *A Midsummer Night's Dream*. Early in the play, Titania describes how her quarrel with Oberon has disrupted the natural world:

"Therefore, the winds, piping to us in vain,
As in revenge, have suck'd up from the sea
Contagious fogs; which falling in the land
Have every pelting river made so proud
That they have overborne their continents:
The ox hath therefore stretch'd his yoke in vain,
The ploughman lost his sweat, and the green corn
Hath rotted ere his youth attain'd a beard;
The fold stands empty in the drowned field,
And crows are fatted with the murrion flock;
The nine men's morris is fill'd up with mud,
And the quaint mazes in the wanton green
For lack of tread are undistinguishable:
The human mortals want their winter here;
No night is now with hymn or carol blest:

118 see for example Lewis Spence, *British Fairy Origins*.

Therefore, the moon, the governess of floods,
Pale in her anger, washes all the air,
That rheumatic diseases do abound:
And thorough this distemperature we see
The seasons alter: hoary-headed frosts
Far in the fresh lap of the crimson rose,
And on old Hiems' thin and icy crown
An odorous chaplet of sweet summer buds
Is, as in mockery, set: the spring, the summer,
The childing autumn, angry winter, change
Their wonted liveries, and the mazed world,
By their increase, now knows not which is which:
And this same progeny of evils comes
From our debate, from our dissension;
We are their parents and original."[119]

Summarising this in one phrase, Titania later tells Bottom that: "I am a spirit of no common rate:/ The summer still doth tend upon my state."[120]

These are vivid descriptions of the woes that can befall Nature if the fairies do not lend their guiding hand and support. We know, too, from other sources, of their powers to control the weather, whether this relates to mermaids, pixies or Scottish hags.[121] Most often in accounts we find these powers wielded to punish or harm humans who have in some way offended or violated fairy kind, but it must follow that they are able to influence the seasons and the sprouting and ripening of crops.

---

119 Act II, scene 1.
120 Act III, scene 1.
121 See my *Beyond Faery* for more on this.

A Midsummer Night's Dream also makes clear that the fairies influenced *human* fertility as well.[122] It seems clear, then, that earlier generations understood that the fairies controlled the natural world and that, as a result, they could bring either prosperity or ruin to communities. Given this power, their propitiation was fundamental to life and health. We see instances of this from all around the British Isles. In one case, a Dartmoor sheep farmer's flock was plagued by disease. He concluded that the only way of saving his stock and his livelihood was to go to the top of a tor and there to sacrifice a sheep to the pixies – a move which promptly alleviated the problem.[123]

At Halloween, the population of the Hebridean island of Lewis would attend a church ceremony that included pouring ale into the sea in the hope that the sprite called 'Shony' *(Seonaidh)* would guarantee a good supply of seaweed in the year ahead; so too on the remote isle of St Kilda, where shells, pebbles, rags, pins, nails and coins were thrown into the sea. Seaweed may not seem very important to most of us today, but it was a vital fertiliser and source of winter fodder for cattle, so a plentiful supply of 'sea ware' on the beaches was essential to survival. This is nicely demonstrated by the story of a ghillie of the MacDonald clan on the Isle of Skye who saw a *bean nighe* (a type of banshee) washing a shroud at Benbecula. He crept up behind her and seized her, thereby entitling himself to three wishes. That of all the things he chose was a guarantee that the loch near his home would be full of seaweed indicates the significance of humble kelp to the economy.

---

122 Act V, scene 2.
123 V. C. Clinton-Baddeley, *Dartmoor,* London: A & C Black, 1925, 97.

Other Scottish examples of the influence of the supernatural over the health and fertility of livestock are to be found in the widespread habit of offering milk to *glaistigs, urisks* and *gruagachs*. These creatures have a direct influence upon the wellbeing of farm animals and cheating or neglecting them could only lead to ruin.[124]

Something similar is seen in England, too, in respect of fruit and nut trees. English orchards are haunted by sprites whose role is to bring life to the trees and to protect the crop from thefts. These faeries go by various names, Owd Goggy, Lazy Lawrence, Jack up the Orchard, the grig and the apple tree man. At harvest time, a few apples should always be left behind for them – an offering called the 'pixy-word' (or hoard) – and, if this is offering is made, the faeries will bless the crop. It's also known that the pixies make their own cider: they have been heard pounding the apples (and grinding their corn) underground at Sheep's Tor on Dartmoor.[125]

FAIRIES IN THE CORN FIELDS

It's often reported that the fairies bake their own bread – bread of superlative flavour – and of course the grain for that has to come from somewhere. The fairies grow and harvest their own crops – as proved by a Welsh story of a human ploughman who was asked by fairies to mend their plough for them. The grain and flour the fairies use is not all stolen, by any means, although there are plenty of stories from across England of

---

124 see *Beyond Faery,* 2020.
125 *The Standard,* July 24th 1873, 4– 'Dartmoor;' see too my book *Faery.*

fairies filching corn, grain by grain, from granaries. Whilst on the island of Islay, it's said that the local fairies claim the top grain from every stalk – and will have harvested it well before the farmer enters the field with his scythes. Scottish poet Robert Buchanan, in his poem *The Faëry Reaper*, alleges that the faeries can only sow and reap their harvest at night and with the help of a virgin human girl.[126]

Some fairies seem to play some sort of protective role towards human crop cultivation, being almost like minor agricultural deities. On the Isle of Man, the link between the good neighbours and prosperity was explicit: Walter Gill was told that the dying out of (belief in) the phynoderee over the previous century had led to a decline in Manx agriculture. At the very least, the fairies may assist agrarian farming in material ways. In Staffordshire, it was believed that the local fairies would help to find and return items lost from ploughs, such as iron pins, the reward for which would be a piece of cake and a bottle of ale.[127]

As just mentioned, across England, there's a host of sprites whose sole function seems to be guarding orchards, fruit bushes and nut groves from the depredations of thieves and children. From Scotland, we have the curious tale of 'Jeanie's Granny' about a fairy who performs this same function in the fields. When she was a child, Jeanie's grandmother got up one night to steal some newly harvested grain so as to feed her horse. When she got to the fields, however, she saw a tiny woman hopping from stook to stook; the child became scared

---

126 Rhys, *Celtic Folklore*, 64; Buchanan, 'Faery Reaper', *Ballads of Life, Love, and Humour*, 1882.
127 Gill, *Manx Scrapbook*, 1929, c.IV; E. Cope, *Memorials of Old Staffordshire*, 1909, 'Some local fairies'.

and ran home without taking any corn. In another story from Dartmoor, a man was annoyed to find that all his stooks of harvested corn were disturbed overnight. He decided to watch the following night to see what the cause might be and, just as he had suspected, pixies appeared and began to pull all the stooks into one corner of the field. Very possibly this was being done by them as the first stage of building a rick, but the pixies were too small to make a good job of it and the farmer interrupted them – at which point they vanished (they might alternatively have been preparing to steal the crop, which would have been much more in character: in a story from Ardnamurchan in the Highlands, a man outwitted the fairies who'd been reaping his crop at night by leaving a wise old man in the field. When fairies appeared and started to harvest the grain, he then counted their number out loud and by this simple means banished them forever).[128]

The strange relationship of fairies to arable crops is also found in an account of the harvest customs of Westruther parish in Berwickshire. When harvesting began, it was held to be very bad luck to cut a snail in half with the first stroke of the sickle or scythe. If this happened, the worker had to go home, saying that their blade was blunt and wouldn't cut anything. The reasoning behind this was that the fairies danced in the stubble fields and, if they were surprised by the early arrival of the harvesters in the morning, they would hide themselves in the shells of snails. Cutting the snail, therefore, meant that a fairy would have placed a spell on your tool for the rest of that day. To express sorrow, the only option for the worker was to go home and, the next day, to work with much

---

128 Campbell, *Superstitions*, 54.

greater care. If they followed these rules, they would enjoy a very lucky day instead.[129]

Whilst there is evidence that crops are raised by the fairies, it is not so clear how they subsequently process and prepare them. In the Buchan district of Scotland, the local fairies would use people's barns at night to thresh their corn, presumably because they did not have suitable structures themselves (barns are designed to have a through draught between two doors so as to blow chaff away from grain; living under hills, the faes would clearly lack such arrangements). This tendency to commandeer others' property could rebound against them though. It was said that, if you could enter a barn and seize the flail before the head stopped wagging, the fairies would be obliged to help thresh your grain as well. The snag was, naturally, that they were too quick to be caught out. There is a story from Cleitinn, outside Pitlochry, that even suggests that the local fairies were operating their own mill there. If you left a sack of grain outside in the evening, by the next morning it would have been ground for you, with the miller's customary share of the flour taken, just like a human miller. In contrast to this evidence of fairy industry, there are as often stories of men being asked to mend broken kitchen implements (baking peels especially) there are just as many stories of the fays approaching human households seeking to borrow such basic utensils.[130]

Another example of fairy grinding is a Scottish tale from Kirkcudbrightshire in which the fairies ask a miller to leave

---

129 Alice Gomme, 'Collectanea: Harvest Customs,' *Folklore*, vol.13, 1902, 178.
130 Milne, *Myths & Superstitions*, R. Jack, 1891, 17; Dixon, *Pitlochry Past & Present*, 133.

the water wheel in service overnight so that they can enter the mill and grind their corn. At the opposite end of Scotland, in the Buchan district, the local fairies ground their oats in mills, a practice which was believed to be lucky for the miller. If the fairies were heard grinding at night, the miller would gather up the dust and flour left the next morning to ensure good fortune. In fact, one miller rather cynically stopped his wheel from turning one night and, after the fairies had discovered they could not mill their grain, he appeared and 'mended' the gears, being rewarded with a small amount of meal which, if pressed into the corners of his meal bin, would give a never-ending supply for seven years. Mutual accommodation and respect lie at the heart of these arrangements. A Breadalbane miller, hearing the fairies at work in his mill one night, merely opened the door and asked "Take care of wood, iron and stone, and remember to keep my dues." Then he left the fairies to it, but found the next morning that they had left a wooden dish of meal, a supply that proved never to diminish (until his wife remarked wonderingly upon it). Just the same as in Scotland, the ferish of the Isle of Man are widely known to use mills at night.[131]

More frequently, though, the fairies seem reliant upon humans to get tasks done. That said, this need not necessarily imply helplessness, as fairy cunning can still come into play. A Devonshire man called Robin found that his threshing never decreased. He decided to watch his barn one night and discovered that the local pixies were bringing grain into his barn, surreptitiously getting him to thrash their corn for

---

131 Campbell, *Popular Tales,* 66, 81 & 414; Milne, *Myths & Superstitions of the Buchan District,* 17; J. MacDiarmid, 'Fragments of Breadalbane Folklore,' *Transactions of the Gaelic Society of Inverness,* vol.26, 1905, 37.

them. He chased them off and they never took advantage of him again; instead, whenever Robin was out poaching, they would terrify him by appearing as a very bright light, making him think that the gamekeeper had caught him.[132]

Accepting that the faes do grow their own grain, what is far from clear is the productiveness of fairy farming. A regular feature of traditional folk stories – especially in Wales and Scotland – is the fairy woman who visits a human home to beg for a little flour or oatmeal. This implies food shortages in faery – though it might be observed that these accounts are often associated with more marginal arable areas where the human population could well have faced similar dearths. We should also note that the return of the meal borrowed is a constant feature of these stories. Settling debts is central to fairy morality and, in addition, they often do more than that: as well as restoring the measure of flour taken, a spell will be cast on the human store so that it is never empty thereafter. Apparently, this is a benefit the fairies can't grant themselves.[133]

In contrast to suggestions of fluctuating food supplies, there's the evidence of the feasts and banquets that are frequently seen, which hardly suggests starvation. Isobel Gowdie of Nairn, a Scottish woman tried for witchcraft in April 1662, reported that she had visited the queen of fairie under the Deunie Hills. Not only was the fairy court surrounded by alarming elf-bulls, but Isobel was given meat (food) by the queen – more than she could eat.

---

132 Northcote, 'Devonshire Folklore,' *Folklore,* vol.11, 1900, 214.
133 an example story is in Cromek, *Remains of Nithsdale & Galloway Song,* 300.

GARDEN GNOMES

We also come across lots of fairies working in gardens, in green houses and in vegetable patches. These are the beings often described as gnomes and it seems that their dedication to plant life is so great that they will cultivate human plots merely for the satisfaction of seeing healthy fruit and vegetables. The most curious story comes from West Yorkshire from about 1850. A man called Henry Roundell of Washburn Dale near Harrogate got up early to hoe the weeds in his crop of turnips. When he reached his field, he was astonished to discover every row being hoed by a host of tiny men in green, all of them singing shrilly. As soon as he entered the field, they fled like scattered birds. Most often they will be gardening or cultivating and they've been sighted digging, with a rake, tidying up leaves and twigs or with a wheelbarrow.[134]

DAIRY FAIRIES

There's a definite close association between fairies and cattle – and that may not be just because they want to consume their milk and cream. For example, William Bottrell recounts the story of Rosy, the fine red milk cow of the Pendar family of Baranhual Farm in Penwith. She gave twice the milk of the other cows, but would often disappear from the farm in the evenings. Eventually, Molly the milkmaid discovered the reason: a four-leaf clover was included in the pad of herbs she used to carry the milk pail on her head and it enabled her to see that the cow was surrounded by

---

134 Roberts *Folklore of Yorkshire*, Stroud: History Press, 2013, 60.

dancing fairies, who were taking turns to milk her and stroking and tickling the beast in between. The cow was evidently very happy in their company. The farmer's wife decided to wash the cow's udders in brine to terminate the fairy thefts, but the only result was that Rosy ceased to give any milk at all.

A related account from Sutherland in the far north of Scotland is the reminiscence of an old woman who, as a small girl, had gone out with her mother one summer evening to tend the cows in the field. She was able to see small green people playing near the cattle, although her mother saw nothing.[135]

As stated at the start, there's a definite affinity between the little people and cows which benefits the milk yield. In Staffordshire, it's also believed that the local fairies help the farmers by preventing hedgehogs sucking the cows' milk at night, a habit for which hedgehogs were once thought to be notorious. On Westray in Orkney, it was believed that, at calving time, milk should be offered to the local fairies (or trows) by pouring it into a hole in the top of a fairy hillock at Muilie. It seems from this that the fairies had some role overseeing and protecting the heifers and their offspring.[136]

The Welsh evidence is that the fairies (certainly the *tylwyth teg*) have extensive and handsome herds of cattle. A frequent element in Welsh stories is of cattle that have been brought to a marriage with a human, or have interbred with a human farmer's herd, which are then called back to Faery as the result of some perceived or real insult – such as deciding to slaughter one. They will be summoned each by name, evoking their qualities and their value to human and fairy farmers:

---

135 G. Sutherland, *Folklore Gleanings,* Wick: John O'Groats Journal, 1937, 22.
136 E. Cope, *Memorials of Old Staffordshire,* 1909, 'Some local fairies;' *Old Lore Miscellany, Orkney and Shetland,* vol.2, 1908, 22.

"Brindled cow, white speckled,
Spotted cow, bold freckled,
The four-field sward mottled,
The old white-faced,
And the grey Geingen,
With the white bull,
From the court of the King,
And the little black calf,
Though suspended on the hook,
Come thou also, quite well, home.
The four grey oxen,
That are on the field
Come you also,
Quite well home."[137]

The cows may be individually named, or they might be identified by particular features, such as a lack of horns, but they are each valuable and respected by the fairy herder.

FARM LABOURING FAIRIES

Quite a number of British fairy types are known for their readiness to labour on human farms, usually in return for warmth by the fire, a modest helping of food and (sometimes) some clothes. These groups include the hobgoblins, brownies, boggarts, pucks and fynoderees, all of which have been known to put to their considerable strength and stamina at the disposal of mortal masters. The most famous of these is

---

137 Rhys, *Celtic Folklore*, 10, 144 & 149.

Robin Good-fellow, a hob so synonymous with agricultural work that he is usually depicted with a flail or a broom. Surprisingly, despite their reputation for being small in stature, even Exmoor pixies have been known to labour in the fields and barns.[138]

The classic farming fairy of Northern England and Lowland Scotland is the domestic brownie or *broonie*, who will undertake all the tasks necessary to run a human smallholding. These creatures will tend the farmers' cattle and sheep, milk the cows, reap the crops, thresh the grain and involve themselves in all other aspects of processing the produce of the farm, such as helping in a mill. They will even keep an eye on the human servants and labourers. Brownies are diligent and untiring workers, but they expect to receive a share of all farm produce, such as butter, beer and milk and (as is widely known) they can be driven off by slights, perceived or real. A brownie at Invergarry was accidentally scalded by a servant and left the farm, taking all the prosperity with him. Most notoriously, these naked creatures can be repelled by providing them with clothes.[139]

Brownies help out on a permanent basis with farming tasks, but other fairy types can be recruited to provide 'temporary labour' in times of need. From North-East Scotland there's the story of the 'Red Cappies' who were called on to assist

138 Snell, *Book of Exmoor*, 1903, 254.
139 Stoddard, *Remarks on Local Scenery*, London: William Miller, 1801, 64; Stewart, *Shetland Fireside Tales*, Lerwick: T & J Manson, 1923, 134; Douglas, *Scottish Fairy & Folk Tales*, New York: A. L. Burt Company, 1901, 177; Heron, *Observations Made in a Journey*, Perth: W. Morison, and Glasgow: John Murdoch, 1799, 227; *New Statistical Account of Scotland*, vol.3, Edinburgh & London: W. Blackwood & Sons, 1845, 260; M. Martin, *A Description of the Western Isles of Scotland*, London: Andrew Bell, 1716, 391.

with threshing grain. Generally, across the Highlands you'll find the Gaelic tradition of the *ceaird-chomuinn* ('association craft') whereby people can be endowed with particular skills by the faes, such as the ability to undertake prodigious feats of ploughing, sowing and harrowing. The recipient is offered two choices: to have either 'ingenuity without advantage' or 'advantage without ingenuity'. One will be clever and highly skilled, but will never be rich; the other will make the man prosperous, but he will be stupid. Even great skill in thieving can be granted, apparently.[140]

Sometimes, too high a price can be demanded for receipt of great skill. On Skye, two banshees once blinded a man they found asleep outside (we don't know why they did this – perhaps he was on a fairy hill); in compensation they gave him unrivalled ability as a piper and a fairy chanter for his pipes. A similar tale is told of Peter Waters of Caithness, who met a fairy woman at a well. She apparently spontaneously offered to endow him with great prowess, either as a preacher or playing the bagpipes. He chose to be a piper and she even gave him a set of pipes. All she asked was that, in return, they meet again after seven years. In the meantime, he won great fame and fortune for his music but when he returned to meet her at the well one moonlit night seven years later, he was never seen again. In a third account, a young woman was struggling to learn to spin and weave, but lacked any natural ability at the crafts. One night she wished that someone would help her and, sure enough, a fairy woman appeared and offered to teach her – the price being her first-born child unless the girl could guess the fairy's name. The girl became

---

140 J. G. Campbell, *Superstitions*, 159 & 181.

a great cloth maker, as promised, and – as in so many fairy stories, including *Tom Tit Trot* – she eventually also managed to overhear the *bean-sith's* name and saved her child.[141]

Over and above the familiar Lowland *broonies*, there's a host of other (Highland) Scottish beings with strong farming connections. Many of these are particularly linked to the pastoral economy of this upland region. The *gruagach* is a generally kindly being that looks after the cattle of a farm or a village, for which duties she receives a daily bowl of whey or a regular offering of milk poured out over a holed stone or special slab of rock. As well as her care for the livestock, the *gruagach* will perform labouring tasks such as threshing. Like many of her kind, if she's offered clothes, she'll desert a farm and if her regular helping of milk is forgotten, she'll wreak havoc, beating people with her staff, turning the cows into the crops and such like.[142]

Also intimately associated with cattle is the *glaistig*, a being often portrayed as a malevolent and violent hag, but whose more benign aspect is as a dairy maid and cow-herd. She is a solitary creature who is seldom seen but is often heard, using her powerful voice to keep the cattle in check. *Glaistigs* are said to be human women who are subject to fairy enchantment and so have some fairy powers. For this reason, the *glaistig* can sometimes shape-shift into the form of a dog to better herd and protect the livestock. She expects a pail of milk nightly and will react angrily if this is withheld or forgotten. In some places,

141 Campbell, *Superstitions*, 139 & 147; Calder, *Sketch*, 48.
142 MacDougall & Calder, *Folk Tales*, 217; Campbell, *Superstitions*, 184; *New Statistical Account of Scotland*, vol.14, 1845, 275; T. Pennant, *A Tour in Scotland*, London: B. White, 1790, 359; S. Johnson, *A Journey to the Western Isles*, Edinburgh: Lawrie & Symington, 1774, 151.

milk is also offered to her at other important points in the farming year, such as when the cattle are first left out overnight each year and when they are brought inside for winter.[143]

In the Highlands, cattle are also tended and farm tasks undertaken by *urisks,* who expect a share of the milk in return. Lastly, the *gunna* is another sort of brownie who cares for cattle at night and keeps them away from cliffs and out of the fields of growing crops. He is never seen except by a person gifted with the second sight. The *gunna* looks like a very thin man dressed only in a fox skin or naked. A person should never respond to this and make the *gunna* clothes – that will simply offend it and drive it away.[144]

A number of other supernaturals are linked to agrarian activities. On Shetland, the *hogboon* is a version of the mainland brownie who undertakes agricultural labouring tasks in return for food. The name derives from the Norse *haugbui,* meaning mound-dweller, because the trows were believed to inhabit the ancient burial mounds. A related being on Orkney is *King Broonie,* a type of trow that particularly took care of a farm's corn. He objected to being watched and, if he felt that he was being spied upon, would scatter the ricks.

Returning to the Scottish mainland, we encounter the *bodachan sabhaill* (the little old man of the barn), a spirit who will help older farmers with their regular tasks, threshing, bundling straw and generally keeping farms in order. They work at night and never play pranks.[145] Lastly, the *urisk* is another brownie-like spirit who lives a solitary life away from

---

143 Campbell, *Superstitions,* 156, 159 & 162; MacDougall & Calder, *Folk Tales,* 267; MacGregor, *Peat Fire Flame,* c.5.
144 Campbell, *Superstitions,* 191.
145 Campbell, *Superstitions,* 188.

humans in wild places during the summer but who in winter will come into farms for warmth and will then undertake farm chores linked to the processing of crops. The *urisk* will grind and thrash grain in return for a bowl of cream and other treats. They are very strong and clever and can be savage if provoked – usually by a human presuming to speak to him. The presence of an *urisk* is said to be a sign of prosperity and a promise of comfort; equally, if she becomes unhappy for some reason, the livestock on a farm can all fall ill. The remedy then is for a wise woman to make a ball of oatmeal dough, place it in the mouth of a dog and then feed it to the afflicted cattle.

What is particularly striking about this group of beings is how many of them are semi-wild sprites, often with a parallel reputation for violent acts, and yet they're entrusted with a farm's valuable assets. Of course, the farmers don't recruit them: the faery cowherds are generally inherited or volunteer themselves, but it is nonetheless a curious relationship. The spirit of the wilderness accommodates itself to the human subjugation of the landscape. There is probably a hidden aspect to the commercial transaction, too. Besides acquiring food and shelter, the sprite learns farming skills which may be transmissible to its own community. This is not so much cheap labour, therefore, as an apprenticeship for a farming fay.

Finally, I will note one case from near Holyhead on the Isle of Anglesey (*Ynys Mon*) which is entirely at odds with almost everything that's gone before, both in this section and much of the rest of the text. A Mrs Owen reported to a folklorist in about 1886 that her father had, one night, been threshing in his barn when the *tylwyth teg* appeared and asked him to let them take over the task. He was more than happy to do this (although he probably hesitated to refuse the fairies in any case) so he went in and left them to it. The next morning, he found all the grain threshed, but the fairies had also left him a large sum of money. It seems hard to explain why they would pay to be allowed to perform hard physical labour, unless this payment was either made in recognition of his respect and compliance or, more likely, represented the value of grain which they had taken home with them.[146]

FAIRY THEFTS OF FOOD

As alluded to at the start of this chapter, many faes seem content to subsist upon the farming labour of others. Throughout the British Isles, there are stories of the theft of agricultural produce of all descriptions. For example, a Manx witness described to Evans Wentz how her aunt saw a strange woman appear in the middle of a patch of gorse and then walk right over the top of it to a heifer. She placed her hand on the cow and, within a few days, it had died.[147]

The fairies' mirroring of human commerce described so far seems incongruous when set against what else we know of them: one very notorious fairy trait was to steal human food products (or, at least) the nourishment within them. In his *Secret Commonwealth*, Robert Kirk described how the fairies fed on "the Foyson or substance of Corns and Liquors or corn itself that grows on the Surface of the Earth." As a result, he said, "When we have plenty, they have Scarcity at their Homes," meaning that "We then … do labour for that

---

146 W. Cobb, 'Anglesey Folklore, from near Holyhead,' *Y Cymmrodor*, 1886, vol.7, 197.
147 Evans-Wentz 122.

abstruse People, as well as for ourselves."[148]   Cheese made from milk from which the goodness has been extracted floats like a cork on water, he alleged. In the traditional Scottish ballad *Young Tamlane*, the hero of the title declares that "all our wants are well supplied, From every rich man's store." The fairies' thieving is openly confessed, albeit with a Robin Hood style justification. All the same, it may be understandable why one poet denounced the "sluggish, lazy, thriftlesse elves…"[149]

The fairies stole products from humans by a variety of methods: some more open than others. Boldest of all was to eat food straight off the humans' plates, as happened to Ewan, son of Alasdair Og, of the Dell of Banks on Loch Ericht in Perthshire. He was tending sheep in a lonely bothy and made himself porridge to eat, which he would set aside to cool for a while. Each evening when he came eat, he found it pitted around the edge, as if birds had pecked at it or rain had fallen on the dish. He realised it was the little people stealing his food and he generously (and probably wisely) fashioned small bowls and spoons for them to use when sharing his meal.[150]

In Monmouthshire, the fairies brazenly rustled sheep, cutting them up and dragging them below ground. The same might be achieved with the fairy whirlwind: people could be abducted by catching them up and carrying them off and the same trick worked for sheep on Tiree. Alternatively, the fairies might simply enter a barn and fill a receptacle, or take the cows and milk them overnight. For example, in one story from Fetlar on Shetland, a farmer was riding home past a known trow hill when a voice told him to tell Tüna Tivla that Füna

---

148 Kirk, sections 2 & 3 respectively.
149 William Browne, *The Shepherd's Pipe*.
150 Campbell, *Superstitions*, 73.

Fivla has fallen in the fire and burnt herself. Getting home, he went into his byre and, as he had suspected, found a trow in the process of milking a heifer into a copper pan. He passed on the message and the alarmed mother instantly dropped the pan and rushed home. All at once, he did a good deed for the Grey Neighbours, saved his milk and gained a handy receptacle.[151] This was an especially bold theft – often it was performed in a more stealthy manner: corn, Kirk said, "these Fairies steal away, partly invisible, partly preying on the Grain as do Crowes and Mice." A granary may be emptied, grain by grain or oatcakes may be filched one by one from a hearth.[152]

Sometimes the theft might cause only a temporary loss to the human owner. An animal might be taken and consumed, but it might be magically restored to life afterwards, so that there is no actual loss (although sometimes a bone might be lost in the process, leaving a revived cow that limps).[153] Most frequently, surreptitious and magical means of theft were employed. Milk could be stolen in a hazel switch; it could be bewitched away by burying a cow's hair under a stall in the byre, by touching the pot chain of the cow's owner or by obtaining the horse-hair teether used to secure the cow during milking.[154] To steal milk the fairies may use by ropes – "What Food they extract from us is conveyed to their Homes by Secret Paths, as sume skilfull Women do the Pith and Milk from their Neighbours

151 Wherry, 'Miscellaneous Notes from Monmouthshire,' *Folklore,* vol.16, 1905, 63; Haldane-Burgess, 'Some Shetland Folklore,' *Scottish Review,* vol.25, 1895, 96; Campbell, *Superstitions,* 93 & 135.

152 Kirk c.3.

153 Tozer, *Devonshire & Other Original Poems,* Exeter: Devon Weekly Times, 1873, 74.

154 For this and the previous two examples, see Goodrich-Freer, 'The Powers of Evil in the Outer Hebrides,' *Folklore,* vol.10, 1899, 275.

Cows into their own Cheife-hold thorow a Hair-tedder, at a great distance, by Airt Magic…;"[155] or perhaps a magic chain: in Argyll it was said that, on a moonlit night, the fairies would fish an enchanted chain from a pool beneath a waterfall. This chain was dragged through the meadows where the cattle grazed, after which all the milk would go to them.[156]

The fairies might cover their theft by leaving a stock in place of a stolen cow (as in the story, *The Tacksman of Auchriachan*) or by leaving an old man rolled in a cow skin. These stocks can be quite elaborate constructions: a Shetland midwife was attending a birth in a knoll when she saw a fake cow being made out of creels, a mat and rush panniers. This was then left in a field in the semblance of a dead beast.[157]

Rather than stocks, the fairies might alternatively substitute their own cattle, the *crodh sith*, for the human livestock. To the farmer, it would appear as though the entire herd had fallen sick.[158]

Thieving didn't only occur from farms but also at fairs and from market stalls. For example, in Largs in Ayrshire in Scotland it was believed that the fairies would regularly mingle with the crowds and steal yarn and wool from the stalls. The fairies are usually invisible to all but a person who has touched fairy ointment on an eye and who thereby is no longer fooled by fairy glamour. The common punishment for observing the fairies at their nefarious work is loss of sight in the eye affected.[159]

---

155 Kirk c.3.
156 Campbell, *Popular Tales of the West Highlands*, vol.2, 1890, 80.
157 Stewart, *Shetland Fireside Tales*, 7.
158 *Celtic Monthly*, vol.IV, 1895, 55.
159 Campbell, *Superstitions*, 77; Snell, *Exmoor*, 254.

Fairy folk may also be shameless and open about their thefts. An interesting variant of the theme of fairies stealing milk is found in an incident recorded at Brackletter near Lochaber. The fairies stole a farmer's best white dairy cow and, to compound the blatant nature of their theft, they used to bring it back daily to the farm to graze it in his corn field. In the west of Scotland, in Argyll, Tiree and Morvern, the belief was that the fairies took the cows at night to milk them and then would return them to their byres before morning.[160]

The fairies have their own cattle, as we know, and they might sometimes use those to try to lure away a farmer's herd. Once, in the west of Tiree, a herdsman saw a small red cow that was unknown to him in amongst his herd. The other cows seemed to attack it and chase it away, but as it ran off, the rest followed. Soon the red cow reached a large rock and disappeared inside it; the herd would have followed had not the man set to watch them quickly intervened.[161]

Indeed, it seems that for the faes' larceny is as much a source of entertainment as well as material supplies. In Randolph's play *Amyntas* the elves sing that:

"Stolen sweets are always sweeter,
   Stolen kisses much completer,
   Stolen looks are nice in chapels,
   Stolen, stolen are your apples.
   When to bed the world are bobbing,
   Then's the time for orchard robbing;

---

160 Ritchie & Harman, *Exploring Scotland's Heritage: Argyll*, London: HMSO, 1985, 84.
161 Campbell, *Superstitions*, 135.

Yet the fruit were scarce worth peeling
Were it not for stealing, stealing."[162]

The fairies are not to be dissuaded from these habits, because "Fairies, like nymphs with child, must have the things they long for." Accordingly, they pilfer dairy products, fruit and anything else that takes their fancies. For instance, if they find people at a feast, they may adopt a disguise to scare off the revellers just so that they may get their hands on the dainties.[163] It might reasonably be proposed that this trait is a fundamental characteristic of fairy kind: "Elves, urchins, goblins all and little fairies that do filch."

SUMMARY

In conclusion, although our tendency is to imagine carefree and pleasure-loving fairies, the reality is often more complex. They grow their own food, like any community must, and many are very hard working – even on behalf of human kind and in return for quite informal arrangements as to recompense.

---

162 Act III, scene 4.
163 *Robin Goodfellow's Merry Pranks.*

Harvesting the Wild

Fairies are, predominantly, rural dwelling beings. This means that, as well as cultivating their own crops and livestock, they are extremely well placed to be able to harvest the bounty of the natural environment.

HUNTING

Foodstuffs aren't just cultivated. Wild beasts and birds can also be exploited and there is good evidence to show that fairies enjoyed the hunt. It may have been primarily an aristocratic pastime, but it could nonetheless supplement the supplies to the kitchen.

Medieval poems describe the fairies out on horses hunting in the forests. For this they needed hounds as well, and the poems mention 'hundes berkyng' so that it's very clear that specially bred dogs for the chase were available. In the poem, *Sir Orfeo*, the knight meets the royal fairy court out on the chase, each rider bearing a falcon on the hand. They went hawking by a river and, as the water fowl rose up, the hawks pounced and slew them. "Of game thai founde wel gode haunt," the poet wrote – mallards, heron and cormorant. The quality of fairy hunting hounds is attested to in one Scottish story, 'The Maidens,' in which two fairy women take a liking for a young human hunter and give him a new hunting dog. It is so excellent that nothing ever escapes it.[164]

On the Isle of Man, repeated sightings confirm that the particular pleasure of the island fairies was hunting with horses and packs of hounds. They have been encountered dressed up in green coats with flat red caps with much cracking of whips, blowing of horns and yelping of dogs. Fairy hunts have also been sighted in Wales and, in Sutherland in the north of Scotland, it's said that the fairies hunt three or four times weekly, riding to the sound of fifes.[165]

We get a closer view of a fairy hunting party from a story told on the island of Benbecula. Two men were tending calves one night at Nunton, a place known in Gaelic as Baile-na-Caileach, 'the Hag's Fort'. Suddenly, two dogs rushed into their hut, both on silver jewelled leashes. The dogs ran around, scaring the cows, until a voice was heard outside calling to the greyhounds by their names, 'Slender Fay, Mountain Traveller, Black Fairy, Lucky Treasure, and Grey Hound (*Sitheach-seang, Siubhal-bheann, Dubh-sith, Cuile-rath, Cu-gorm*)'. They were told to 'seek beyond' and, at that command, they ran out again. The men followed, and saw bright figures in the sky with hounds and hawks, and music like bells filling the air.[166]

These pleasures had a practical contribution to the fairy economy, therefore, but they came at a cost too: someone had

---

164 MacDougall & Calder, *Folk Tales & Fairy Lore*, 285 'Na Gruagaichean;' see the poems *Sir Orfeo* and *Thomas of Erceldoune*.
165 Roeder, *Manx Folk Tales*, 5, 7 & 8; Waldron, *Description of the Isle of Man*, 33; Dempster, 'Folklore of Sutherlandshire,' *Folklore Journal*, vol.6, 1888, 219.
166 Carmichael, *Carmina Gadelica*, vol.2, 257–8.

to care for the mounts and the hounds; someone had to train them to their tasks. Masters of hounds and falconers all need wages and accommodation.

FAIRY FISHING FLEETS

The Manx faeries in particular excel at the many crafts associated with fishing. They have been seen boat building at Perwick (although one commentator dismissed this as mere imitation of humans). Given that the boats have been seen in use, this seemed unfounded. In addition, they have been spotted engaged in other preparations, such as mending nets and making barrels to store the catch of herring in. At Cronk-ny-Irree-Laa near Patrick, there's a cave called Ooig-ny-Sieyr (the Cooper's Cave) in which the fairy barrel makers were regularly heard at work. It's believed that to hear them (especially in May) promises good herring fishing for the fairy fleets. However, good catches for the fairies can mean poor fishing for humans, and vice versa. Also, it's believed that to see their boats, or rather the innumerable twinkling lights of them, at sea is either a sign that a good catch may be found there – or a warning to put in, for it heralded a storm. Clearly their knowledge of sea and weather were greatly to be trusted.[167]

---

167 Gill, *Second Manx Scrapbook*, c.III; *Yn Lioar Mannanagh* vol.4, 161; Morrison, *Manx Fairy Tales*, 1911, 'Little footprints;' *Manx Notes & Queries*, no.205; Gill, *Third Manx Scrapbook*, c.3; S. Morrison, 'Manx Dialect Connected with Fairies,' *Proceedings of the Isle of Man Natural History and Archaeological Society*, New Series vol.1, 1906.

The fairies' boats have been seen on beaches after they have returned from a fishing trip and also being hauled to safety before a storm. Their fleets are sometimes seen out at sea in Peel Bay, illuminated by lanterns, although hearing the sound of rowing and the splash of their oars is more common because they will tend to extinguish their lights if they realise human boats are near.[168]

Although the best sources on fairy fisheries are from the Isle of Man, it was not exclusive to the island. For instance, in the north east of Scotland, the fairy fishing boats were often seen heading out to sea on fine summer mornings.[169] In all these cases, we must also reflect upon the fact that the sailors need to get their boats from somewhere, a fact that implies that either they, or specialists within their community, are capable boat builders. The iron making needed to supply nails, anchors, hooks and suchlike will be discussed later. Fairy woodsman will also need to fell trees and then prepare and process the timber for the construction of these vessels.

FAIRY FISHERMEN

As well as marine waters, fairies take fish from rivers and lakes. There is witness evidence to confirm their liking for trout at least. They also will take steps to conserve the fish stocks, so that humans caught trying to catch fish at spawning time are

---

168 *Yn Lioar Mannanagh* vol.III, 482; *Manx Notes and Queries*, 1904, 131; Morrison, *Manx Fairy Tales*, 1911, 'Little footprints'; *Manx Notes & Queries*, no.205; Roeder, *Manx Folk Tales*, 'Fairies of Sea & Shore.'
169 Walter Gregor, *Notes on the Folklore*, 65.

likely to have an alarming encounter with a supernatural being such as a bogie that teaches them a lesson for the future.[170]

There could, inevitably, be competition between humans and fairies for the best fishing grounds. In this conflict, the fae folk naturally had unfair advantages as they could use their powers of glamour. On the River Tweed in Scotland, it was the custom to impregnate the nets with salt – and to scatter the water itself with salt – so as to blind the fairies and prevent them cheating the snares. George Fenwick reported that he had seen this done at Coldstream in March 1879.[171]

DEER

Given their well-known liking for milk, cream and butter, it's unsurprising that the Good Folk keep their own herds for milking. In the Scottish Highlands, the fairies were especially associated with the red deer and, indeed, it was believed around Lochaber and Mull that the deer were their only cattle. One Gaelic fairy lullaby that has been recorded goes like this:

> "On milk of deer I was reared,
>   On milk of deer nurtured,
>   On milk of deer beneath the ridge of storms,
>   On crest of hill and mountain."[172]

---

170 Johnson, *Seeing Fairies*, San Antonio: Anomalist Books, 2014, 25; Goodrich-Freer, 'Powers of evil in the Outer Hebrides,' *Folklore*, vol.10, 1899, 273–74.
171 *Folklore Record*, vol.2, 1879, 209.
172 Carmichael, *Carmina Gadelica*, vol.2, 232.

From this it seems that fairy babies might well be fed upon deer milk. It was also alleged that fairy women could transform themselves into deer and might be captured in this guise; the Scottish ballad *Leesom Brand* concerns a fairy woman who has some mysterious vital link with white hinds. A story from Glen Etive even tells of a woman abducted by the fairies who was recovered after she was seen running free with the deer in the glen. Some people go further and say that these fairy women become the lovers of hunters and help them in the chase.[173]

Of course, if the deer comprise the fairies' herds, there will be inevitable conflict with humans who wish to hunt them for venison. For this reason, it is also believed that the fairies will use their powers of glamour to keep their herds hidden from human eyes. For this reason, it is very rare to find the carcases of deer that have died of old age or to find their shed horns. Despite this risk of depredation, it is said that the fae woman called the Carlin of the Red Stream was able to revive any of her deer that had been caught and slaughtered, as long as she could obtain some of the flesh and taste the juice of the meat.[174]

Certain hags and fay women herd wild deer just like cattle. The supernatural woman called the *cailleach* has been seen on Mull, driving her deer along the beaches to graze seaweed during winter. Another hag, called the *Cailleach Bheinn a Bhric* pastured her deer in Glen Nevis. She would milk them there, singing as she did so, and hunters would blame her for concealing the animals from them if they were unable to find any. Conversely, she might in certain cases allow a deer to be

173 Campbell, *Superstitions,* 90, 110 &123; Child Ballad no.15.
174 Campbell, *Superstitions,* 133.

taken. The story is told of a man called Murdoch who was stalking deer in Gaick Forest when he came across a fairy woman milking her hinds. She had some green yarn over her shoulder and one of the deer snatched this and swallowed it. The fairy slapped the animal and wished that Murdoch's bow would fell it. Later, he killed a hind and found the same hank of yarn in its stomach.[175]

A story akin to this last one is told about a young man called Donald of Buinach in Moray. He was renowned as a hunter and for having the second sight. One day, Donald was out with a companion and told his friend to place his foot on top of Donald's; when he did so, he saw a fine herd of deer which had been invisible otherwise – obviously because it had been concealed with fairy glamour. On another occasion, Donald met a *glaistig* who was herding hinds. She told him he took too many hinds, but he excused himself by saying he only took hinds when he couldn't find stags. The fairies might obstruct hunters by other means. A man who had brought down a deer threw it across his shoulders to carry it home, but found it to be immensely heavy. It was only when his companion stuck a knife in the slain animal that the fairies' obstructive spell was dissipated (by the iron blade) and the body resumed its normal weight.[176]

The herds of deer are under fairy protection then, and may be hidden from human sight. Nonetheless, some hunters are favoured and allowed to take what they need, whilst some are taken as lovers by the fairy herders.

---

175 Mackenzie, *Scottish Folklore*, 152; *Celtic Monthly*, vol.16, 1908, 236.
176 MacDougall & Calder, *Folktales & Fairy Lore*, 255; Campbell, *Superstitions*, 134.

Mining Fairies

There's lots of evidence for fairies being just as active as humans in extracting the earth's resources and in manufacturing. This may jar somewhat with the notion of winged flower fairies and rural dwellers, but that convention forgets the fact that gnomes, as first imagined by Paracelsus, are very intimately connected to the mineral riches of the earth. There are also some indications of wider supernatural associations with mines, as in the Cornish account of a pit which was haunted by little black dogs (perhaps related to the 'yeth hounds' of the moors) after an accident took place.[177]

GOING UNDERGROUND

"While the fairies of the mine
Below, shall course the wand'ring beam."[178]

There are two principal industrial activities in which fairies are involved. These are metal working and mining. The fays mine for both coal and ores and they have been associated with the tin mines of the south west of England, the lead

---

177 *Guernsey Star,* Feb. 10th 1885, 4 'Animal Ghosts.'
178 Henry Boyd, *Poems,* Dublin: Graisberry & Campbell, 1793, 532.

mines of the Long Mynd in Shropshire and with the copper mines of Cumberland and North Yorkshire.

There are two principal types of mine fairy – the knockers of the south west of England (also called 'nuggies', 'bockles', 'gathons' or 'buccas') are very well known. In the coal and metal ore mines of Wales, we find the *coblynau* (i.e. goblins) and the *espryd y mwyn* (mine spirits). Other named mine spirits are the Blue-Cap of the Northumberland coalmines, a very strong being who moved the wheeled coal tubs on the underground railways, and the Cutty Soams of County Durham, who were mine bogles, known for their vengeful mischief – which included such pranks as cutting the traces (or 'soams') on the underground coal wagons, much to the annoyance and inconvenience of the young girls whose lot it was to drag them through the dark tunnels.

Despite the differing regional names, it seems safe to treat most of these beings as one underground species. The knockers and *coblynau* are very hard-working sprites who are frequently heard but very seldom seen; the sounds of their picks, their wheelbarrows and the falls of stone that they cause may be heard deep in mines. Occasionally they may be spotted working or lounging near the entrances to shafts, and those who have seen them describe beings the size of a one or two-year-old child (about eighteen inches high), with large heads and ugly old men's faces; they are dressed just like human miners. Blue Cap apparently has no physical form, but his presence is indicated by a light blue flame which settles on the wagons he moves. The other exception is the mine pixy 'gathon' (if Mrs Bray is to be believed, at any rate). She describes him as naked and fat, with large ears and a long bushy tail.[179]

The mine sprites have diminutive tools and equipment matching that of the human miners and they labour tirelessly – digging, transporting and winding their coal and ore to the surface. In the masque, *The Fairies' Farewell*, presented at Coleorton on Candlemas Day 1618, we hear a further description of the fairies' labours:

"blacke faeries ... ye dancing spiritts of the Pittes: ... helpe them hole & drive sharp theire Picks & their moindrils, keepe away the dampe & keepe in theire Candles, draine the Sough & hold them out of ye hollows..."

At Llanferris, near Mold in North Wales, a miner once saw a little man climbing out of an abandoned human mine working. He was dressed just like a mortal miner, with a tiny pickaxe and other equipment, but when he had reached the top of the ladder, he disappeared at a hedge. The mine had been worked out, but further prospecting revealed there to be ore still present, albeit not in commercial quantities. Even so, it was apparently worth the fairies' while to excavate there. The same report described the 'frolicsome' nature of these Flintshire mine fairies; they were often heard laughing, especially at Christmas, and would sometimes guide men to good veins.[180] A late Victorian description of the Welsh mine sprites described how the sound of their boring, blasting and loading would lead miners to seams of coal or veins of ore but that, once the men had located the minerals, the sprites would cease to work.[181]

---

179 Bray, *Peeps at Pixies*, 10.
180 *Bye Gones*, 1882–83, 340.
181 *Weekly Mail*, April 25th 1891, 9– 'Welsh Superstitions.'

In contrast to these narratives, Wirt Sykes claimed that all this frenetic subterranean labour was just for show but accomplished nothing at all. The writer of *A Pleasant Treatise of Witches* (1673) explained that this was done because these mine elves "busy themselves chiefly in imitating the operations men ... these seem to laugh, to be cloathed like workmen, to dig the earth, and to do many things they do not, mocking sometimes the workmen but seldome or never hurting them."[182]

These views might be correct – or it might instead be the case that human observers never saw any evidence of tangible results in this world. Blue-Cap is the exception here, as he assisted the human miners and, perfectly reasonably, expected to be paid for his work at the same rate as every other 'putter' who moved the coal around the tramways. Rather like fairies borrowing flour from householders, he insisted upon being given the exact agreed sum and would refuse underpaid wages or leave behind any surplus. Evidently, Blue Caps were *not* brownies and neither toiled for free nor accepted very modest payment in kind.

Though often heard at night (in the North Yorkshire lead mines this earned them the name of the 'Ghostly Shift'), these spirits never worked in the mines on Saturdays or on Christian holidays and, in respect for this, the miners too would avoid working on the same days. The sprites also objected to whistling and to use of the sign of the cross, which were therefore proscribed.

---

182 *British Goblins*, 24.

FAIRY AID

The knockers will guide favoured human miners to good seams or lodes by various means. Where no excavation has yet been started, they may indicate promising places to dig. The sprites may dance in rings to indicate spots where men will strike rich ore. Digging wherever a will o' the wisp is seen is also reputed to lead you to a profitable lode. The Reverend Edmund Jones of Gwent gives a very interesting account of a version of this habit. One morning, a William Evans of Hafod-y-dafel in the parish was crossing the Beacon Mountain when he saw an opencast coal mine where none existed. The fairies were cutting coal, filling sacks and loading horses. This vision is unexplained and, on the face of it, is merely a kind of fairy pantomime, serving no discernible purpose. However, another report from Wales suggests a different interpretation. Lewis Morris, a correspondent of the *Gentleman's Magazine* in 1754, described how, before Esgair y Mwyn lead mine was discovered near Pontrhydfendigaid in Cardiganshire, the local fairies had been observed (and heard) by many people to be hard at work, both day and night. When the mine was established in 1751, though, they disappeared. The same was also the case at Llwyn Llwyd lead mine near Ysbyty Ystwyth, not far from Esgair y Mwyn. These two cases suggest that the Brecon Beacons vision may well have been an indication of a rich coal seam just beneath the surface (a prediction similar to the incident of the fairy railway sighted on the Isle of Man that I mentioned earlier).

Supernatural assistance in finding mineral wealth could sometimes be rather more direct – and detailed. In the mid-nineteenth century, a mine labourer in Mold was visited by a female spirit at midnight. He was asleep in his bed, but she tapped him insistently on his shoulder until he consented to getting up and following her. This ghostly apparition led him to a post where it was indicated that he should start a new mine. So convincing was the information she gave him that he persuaded other men to join him in beginning to dig and, at the time the case was reported in the press, they were forty-two yards deep and confident of soon striking a vein of lead ore. The fairy gave them confidence to carry on because she had described accurately (and with uncanny geological knowledge) the strata they would dig through. What's more, she regularly gave the first miner gold coins as token of her good faith.[183]

Once a new mine has been started, through their tapping underground the fairies point the way to mineral riches. For example, one Cornish tin miner described how he knew he was on the right track to a fruitful lode: "for every stroke of my tool, I heard three or four clicks from the knackers, workan away ahead of me." They will also warn of impending disaster – often by making three distinct knocks against the rock. Generally, then, their presence is welcomed by miners – their noises are not found alarming and it's said to be good luck to see the pixies dancing in the adit of a mine.

The sound of work made by knockers can be prolonged and are not easily explained by other means. For example, at Llwyn Llwyd, voices, blasting, clearing spoil, levelling roadways, boring, pick-axeing and (most notably) pumping were all heard – when there were no pumps working within a mile of the shafts and when, in any case, pumps were very

---

183 *Cardiff & Merthyr Guardian*, Nov 11th 1850, 4– 'General Miscellany.'

quiet when in operation. Although they may sometimes be heard just once a month or once a year, in 1799 in some mines on Anglesey, the knockers were heard repeatedly over a period of weeks.

FAIRY HINDRANCE

As with all supernatural helpers, the knockers are averse to humans being too inquisitive. Although the sounds of their work indicate how and where to dig, if miners stop their work to listen to the knockers, they will also cease their labours. If they're overlooked, they may pelt stones at the spies – or simply vanish. The sounds of their excavations may point to rich veins of ore – or they may just be mischievous and meant to mislead.

The mine dwarves were well known in the Staffordshire coalfields. They would help the miners and warn them of dangers so long as they weren't too inquisitive; however, if they felt that they had been mistreated or intruded upon, the dwarves would break tools, drop roofs and light the fire damp in revenge.[184]

It's an acknowledged trait of fairies to be mischievous and to play pranks and the subterranean faes are no different in this respect. We've already alluded to the tricks played by the Cutty Soams. Thomas Heywood records them blowing out lamps and stealing tools as well as, far more seriously, untwisting ropes, breaking ladders and raising suffocating damps.[185]

---

184 Burne, 'Staffordshire Folk and Their Lore,' Folklore, vol.7, 1896, 371.
185 Heywood, Hierarchie of Blessed Angels, 568.

As with many fairy types, those who offend the mine spirits (whether with insults or with more direct trespasses), or who try to take advantage of them, will be punished and those miners who betray the source of their good fortune will lose the knockers' favour. At the same time, the sprites claimed a share of human property. This might just be a small portion of the miners' food or of their candle tallow, but there are also accounts of bargains struck whereby the knockers were promised some of the profits of a rich vein in return for guidance locating it. It hardly needs to be said that reneging on such deals would lead to ruin and even death, whilst boasting of fairy aid in finding rich seams of ore will guarantee that the good fortune is lost. Mrs Bray's mine pixy, Gathon, is depicted as a typical prank-playing sprite who has particular objections to miners working on a Sunday, but he also helps the oppressed and the poor, a not uncommon fairy trait.[186]

The fairies may also be found in coal pits; from Scotland we have a report that from time to time they would leave their tiny tools behind as physical evidence of their labours. We also have an account from Derbyshire in the nineteenth century of the colliers of Curbar leaving a share of the coal they had dug for the fairies to ensure good luck.

Miners are a superstitious class of men in any case. The perilous environment within which they work encourages this, as the risk of disaster is ever-present and the need for luck is great. Leicester colliers, for example, said that if they heard the spirits called "the whistlers" pass overhead, they would not go underground because a death had been foretold.

---

186 William Jones, *Credulities of the Past,* London: Catto & Windus, 1880, 131; *Peeps at Pixies,* 10.

This belief combines two faery themes: that of the 'host of the air' and that of prediction of future events by some indirect means.

In some way, then, whether they were mining themselves or simply oversaw the shafts, these varieties of local fairy all had a close interest in the industry.

HEAVY METALS

Despite Sykes' doubts about the productiveness of fairy labours, it seems very reasonable to suppose that ore and coal were extracted and that these formed the raw materials of other enterprises in fairyland.

In *The Secret Commonwealth*, the Reverend Robert Kirk reported that the fairies "strike Hammers, and do such lyke Services within the little Hillocks they most haunt." The trows of Shetland are particularly renowned for their skills working brass, iron and other metals and they have been known to pass on skills such as scythe making to fortunate human children who have been taken to live with them 'under the hill.' A boy abducted by the fairies on Islay – and replaced by a changeling – was eventually freed by his blacksmith father and returned home; it transpired then that he had become expert at forging swords whilst he was away. Highland fairies are said to sit around a fire at night and gossip whilst at the same time they labour "like tinkers" – which surely must imply the manufacture of small domestic items in metal.[187]

---

187 Kirk, *Secret Commonwealth*, chapter 1; J. F. Campbell, *Popular Tales*, no.58; Nicholson, *Folktales*, 21.

It's a curious contradiction that we can have reports of these metalworking abilities at the same time as being repeatedly assured that fairies loath and avoid items made of iron. The only way of reconciling these two accounts is to assume that man-made iron is anathema to them but that their own products, imbued in some way with Faery properties, are harmless. Certainly, we hear of fairies having cutlery for eating and drinking vessels of precious metals – and of course brownies will undertake all sorts of farm tasks for humans – such as reaping corn and hay – that unavoidably involve the use of iron and steel tools.

CONCLUSION

Fairy society is a good deal more complex and more industrious than we might initially assume. Whether they're farming, mining or at market, trading the fruits of those labours, the fays can work just as hard as humans and be just as interested in commerce.

That said, there are those who believe that all this labour is just for show – an imitation of human industry or, even worse, a mockery of it. We have already seen this suggestion being made about the knockers. Of the fairies of lowland Scotland, one writer had this to say:

> "No wise man will either desire their company or their
> kindness. When they come to a house to assist at any work,
> the sooner they are got rid of the better. If hired as servants,
> their wages at first appear trifling, but will ultimately ruin
> their employer. The benefit of their gifts goes ultimately to

themselves or (as they say in Gaelic) 'the fruit of it goes into their own bodies'."

Another authority says of the Scottish brownies that their labour around a farmstead was never sought after and, in fact, most of those who lived with brownies would happily have exorcised them. In the end, then, fairy help to humans is no help.[188]

---

188 E. B. Simpson, *Folklore in Lowland Scotland,* London: J. M. Dent, 1908, 99; *Fraser's Magazine,* vol.25, 1842, 'A Sketch of Scottish Diablerie in General,' 326.

Fairy Industry

We have looked specifically at fairy farming and mining, but there is evidence of a range of other manufacturing and craft activities that are practised in Faery.

Some fairies can be extremely hard workers, dedicated and highly skilled, contrary to what may have been implied in previous chapters. The preparedness of fairies to organise themselves to work together at tasks is demonstrated very well by the many traditional work songs that are recorded. These would be sung by groups of fairy men and women when milking, waulking cloth, rowing or rocking a cradle, for example.[189]

Indeed, they may even take this dedication to hard graft too far. A couple in a cottage on the Isle of Skye were making tweed and incautiously wished that the task was complete (a so-called 'night wish' as mentioned earlier). The fairies came in the night and completed all stages of the lengthy process before the next morning. Then the fairies demanded more work and would not leave until they had been given some. They were asked to roof a barn, a task they again completed in record time, then – in order to get rid of them – they were asked to empty the sea using a sieve. The faes soon realised they had been tricked and abandoned this impossible labour.

---

189 Campbell & Hall, *Strange Things*, 7.

In a very similar story from another part of Skye, a woman wished to herself that her household chores were all completed. Instantly, the fairies appeared and did all the tasks for her. Then they promptly demanded what was to be done next. She asked them to do all the spring work on the farm – the tilling, manuring and such like – and once again this was carried out forthwith – and the fairies asked for more to occupy them. Predictably, the woman was beginning to feel trapped by her good fortune now, so she asked them to fight each other – and obediently they set to. Although this may have got rid of her unwanted helpers, there was a downside, because grass would never grow on the spot where they battled.[190]

CRAFTS

It's been said of the faeries that they are "very ingenious people... very clever, with very skilled artisans." They are gifted in many crafts and, despite some stories to the contrary, highly resourceful and self-reliant.[191]

The faeries are expert weavers, tailors and shoemakers. In the last century or so, in fact, they have increasingly been seen hard at work at various tasks. Prodigious labours are well known for the domestic brownies and hobs, but faes have been seen involved in many other jobs involving physical labour, for example mending a road and transporting burdens – whether in a handcart, in a sack or in buckets suspended from a yoke.

---

190 McCulloch, 'Folklore of the Isle of Skye,' *Folklore,* vol.34, 1922, 202 & 206.
191 Grant Stewart *Popular Superstitions,* London: Aylott & Jones, 1823, 73–74.

Whilst leprechauns are known especially as cobblers, they are by no means the only fairies to undertake shoemaking. In one story from Dore in South Yorkshire, a hob thrush features:

> "Once upon a time there was a poor shoemaker who could not earn enough to keep himself and his family. This grieved him very much, but one morning, when he came downstairs, he found a piece of leather which he had cut out already made into a pair of shoes, which were beautifully finished. He sold these shoes the same day, and with the money he bought as much leather as would make two pairs of shoes.
>
> The next morning, he found that this leather too had been made into shoes, but he did not know who had done it. In this way, his stock of shoes kept always getting bigger. He very much wished to know who had made the shoes, so he told his wife he would stay up all night and watch, and then he found Hob Thrust at work upon the leather. As soon as Hob Thrust had finished a pair of shoes the shoemaker took them and put them into a cupboard. Immediately after that, Hob Thrust finished another pair, which the shoemaker also took up and put away. Then he made first one pair of shoes and then another so fast that the little shop was soon filled with them and, as there was no more room in the house, the shoemaker threw the shoes out of the window as fast as Hob Thrust could make them."[192]

---

192 Sidney Addy, *Household Tales,* London: Nutt, 1895, 38.

As with so many stories of fairy aid, with this one there is a sting in the tail. The hob is prodigiously productive and the human ends up with more than he bargained for (perhaps because of his temerity in spying).

The fairies will sometimes apply their craft skills to human tools. At Osebury, on the River Teme in Worcestershire, the tradition is that a broken peel left in a faery's cave there will be mended for you. On the Isle of Orkney, it was believed that, if a spinning wheel was not working well, leaving it out overnight on a faery mound would fix it.[193] The puzzling thing is that it's far more common to hear of fairies seeking to have their goods mended by humans: baking peels, churn-staffs, stools, spades, pails, pick-axes and such like are all regularly broken beyond the skill of their fae owners to repair them.

In the Scottish Highlands, it was believed that – if discovered by a craftsman such as a blacksmith or wheelwright working with the tools of his trade – the fairies can then be compelled to enter into an arrangement called *ceaird chomuinn* (association craft) whereby they will assist in the work whenever required to. The human will simply need to leave unfinished work outside the fairy hillock in the evening and, in the morning, it will be found there completed. The *ceaird* doesn't just apply to manual crafts, in fact, but to farm work and to healing with herbs. As has been described already, though, humans should generally be wary of such transactions. They are seldom entirely one way.[194]

---

193 R. Palmer, *Folklore of Worcestershire* (Hereford: Logaston Press, 2005) 180; Marwick *The Folklore of Orkney* 41; T. Crofton Croker, *Fairy Legends & Traditions* (London: John Murray, 1826) 48.
194 Campbell, *Superstitions of the Highlands & Islands*, 98.

It has been said of the Manx fairies that they are of an imitative disposition. In mines, quarries and boat-building yards they have been heard, and occasionally seen, carrying on the work at night after the men have finished and gone home – but without any noticeable result next morning. In this, the Manx faes differ from the brownie called the fynoderee, of which a man from Maughold said, "You have to do a bit of the work yourself first, to start it, to show them how like, and then they'd go on with it for you." Amongst these mostly invisible bands of fairy workers on the island, the best known are the woodworkers of the Ooig-ny-Seiyr, the Carpenters' (or Coopers') Cave, on the coast near Patrick. Some say they make barrels for the herring fleet, others that they make coffins, but not for themselves. They were heard going at it with unusual vigour before a major disaster befell the boats from Peel.[195]

MAKING STOCKS

There is one handicraft, unique to Faery, at which they excel, and that is the making of 'stocks', false humans and livestock that are used to fool humans into thinking that a person or a cow has not been stolen but has died or is still present, albeit it sick.

This is a craft over which the fairies seem to take great time and pride. I mentioned earlier the fake cows made out of willows and mats; in another Shetland example, a man heard a knocking one day – the sound of someone carving

---

195 Gill, *Third Manx Scrapbook*, c.3.

wood – and when he went to see what was happening, he found some trows carefully shaping a stock to replace his wife. One told the other, "Make it bonnie, because ye ken she's bonnie hersell." Forewarned, he managed to prevent the trows taking his spouse. When he threw the abandoned stock on the fire, it flew up the chimney with a blue flame. Blue flames are characteristic of supernatural beings. Similar attention to detail by the trows led to their failure in a second Shetland case. A farmer's wife had just given birth; he was in his yard working when he heard knocking and voices from his lambing shed. He realised some trows were in there, one of whom said, "Mind the crooked finger." As the farmer's wife had a crooked finger, he knew they must be carving a replica with a view to stealing mother and child. He immediately went into the house and protected his family with an open Bible, a knife and a lit candle. That night he heard a noise in his byre and went out to investigate, armed with the Bible and the steel blade: the trows had been unable to get past his magical protections so they had dropped the stock and left. He kept the lump of wood and used it as a bench in his house.[196]

Stocks are usually made from a piece of timber such as alder or moss oak; the trows of Shetland and Orkney are especially renowned for their artistry in this malign craft. In one account from New Deer in north east Scotland, a man overheard the faeries discussing the stock they were making in the likeness of the local blacksmith's wife. He immediately ran to the couple's house and blessed the woman. A thump was heard outside and, when they looked, a piece of bog fir in

---

196 Nicolson, *Shetland Folklore*, 78; Douglas, *Scottish Fairy & Folk Tales*, 131.

her rough likeness was discovered. For boys and girls, being smaller, a piece of wood might not be needed and instead a cabbage stalk or ragwort stem might be left in the child's place.[197]

For all their glamour, the spell of stocks is easily broken. As we've already seen, if the fairies are interrupted or thwarted in their labours, they may just give up. A Shetland farmer heard a noise in his byre and went to investigate. He found his best cow out of her stall with a rope around her neck, ready to be led away. Taking her back to her pen, he found an identical cow dead on the straw; this was a stock intended to conceal the trows' theft. If a stock is thrown on the fire in a house, it will become animated, shoot up the chimney or out of the smoke hole in the roof and the stolen person or creature will be freed from their faery enchantment and will be able to return home. In one incident from Buckhaven in north east Scotland, the stock jumped from the flames onto the family cat before flying up the chimney.[198]

FAERY BUILDERS

Faeries may from time to time be seen seemingly involved in some sort of construction work (for example, carrying a

---

197 Gregor, *Notes on the Folklore* 62; and see the tale of *Sandy Harry*, Aitken, *Forgotten Heritage* 16; Browne, *History of the Highlands*, Glasgow: A. Fullerton & Co, 1838, 111; Anon, *Folklore & Legends*, 52; Macdiarmid, 'Fragments of Breadalbane Folklore,' *Transactions of the Gaelic Society of Inverness*, vol.21, 1896, 132.

198 Nicolson, *Shetland Folklore*, 79; Haldane Burgess, 'Some Shetland Folklore,' *Scottish Review*, vol.25, 1895, 102; Graham, *Buckhaven*, Stirling: W. Macnie, 1779, 23.

ladder). It is known that they can – if they wish – construct stone towers with their doors, windows and chimneys all skilfully concealed. Indeed, faery-kind seem to excel at constructing grand accommodation for themselves – they've been called "unrivalled architects" whose buildings stand forever.[199] Thomas Keightley recalled a conversation with a young woman in Norfolk who told him that the faeries were a people dressed in white who lived underground where they built houses, bridges and other edifices. Many other accounts of visits to faeryland, such as that by Thomas of Erceldoune, praise the grand castles and palaces they have constructed for themselves.

These faeries were building for themselves in their own realms, but they will interact with humans in construction projects too. There are two situations in which faeries have got involved in building structures in the human world. Firstly, this has occurred under duress. There are several instances where faeries have been compelled, against their will, to carry out tasks for a human. This might happen as the terms of a ransom for a fellow fay or because a human has gained some magical control over the faes. For example, in Scotland a faery queen banished some troublesome elves from Cnoc-n'an-Bocan (Bogle-knowe, or Hobgoblin-hill, near to Menteith) into a spell book, *The Red Book of Menteith*. The condition was that they would only be released when the laird of Menteith opened the volume. Eventually, this happened by mistake and instantly, faeries appeared before him demanding work. Not knowing what work to set them to, his lordship hit upon the plan of making

---

199 see too chapter 4 of my *British Fairies*; Grant Stewart *Popular Superstitions* 77.

a road onto the island where his castle stood. They began the task energetically, but the Earl quickly realised that, if they continued, his hitherto impregnable retreat would be rendered vulnerable to attack, so instead he asked them to make a rope of sand for him. They began this latter task without finishing the former, and finding their new work too much for them, they resolved to abandon it part-done and departed, to the relief of the Earl.

Secondly, a large number of Scottish sites are said to have been built voluntarily by faeries. One, the *Drocht na Vougha* (faery bridge) in Sutherland, was for their own convenience to shorten the journey time around Dornoch Firth; however, it benefited human traffic too and, when one traveller blessed the builders, the bridge sank beneath the waves. Many famous Scottish sites – castles, palaces, bridges and towers – are alleged to have been built by faeries – sometimes in the space of a single night, and sometimes by such laborious means as passing the stones from person to person over a great distance. All this effort to create edifices only used by humans might seem puzzling, but we are told that the church of St Mary's at Dundee was built for gold, so that the Good Neighbours' motivation in these labours might actually be very familiar indeed.

For all their renowned skill, the fairies at the same time seem quite shy of being observed. For example, at Brechin there is a roofless tower (a broch) that was built by 'the Picts' (in other words, the fairies). The walls were erected overnight, but the structure was never finished because a woman looked out at dawn and saw the faery labourers, interrupting them forever. Something very similar was reported to have happened at Crowle in Lincolnshire. There, a man witnessed some fairies mending a road; once again, they vanished, and it was said that they would never finish the job after that intrusion.[200]

It's notable that most of the examples of fairy buildings are Scottish or come from the north of England. It seems that the more northerly faeries are the skilled stone masons, though why this should be we simply can't speculate. Secondly, whilst we can understand why they should wish to build for themselves or hinder building at places to which they had some special attachment, their willingness to work for humans (even for gold) is less comprehensible, especially as that included buildings for religious purposes – something to which they normally violently objected.

What's more, much of the impressive architecture reported by humans during visits to faeryland could have been simply 'glamour' – with no physical reality. We are familiar with stories of midwives taken to assist faery women in labour who believe that they are in fine houses until they accidentally touch their eyelids with ointment intended for the faery new-born and see that, in reality, they are in a ruined building or a cave. Given their magical powers, indeed, one wonders why the Good Folk would bother at all with the labour of actually piling stone on stone when it could (presumably) all be achieved by the wave of a hand (or wand).

FAERY SPINNING

Whilst the Good Folk are said to indulge in several manufacturing enterprises, there is one craft activity that

---

200 D. Black, *History of Brechin*, 1839, 283; Addy, *Household Tales*, 1895, 135.

seems to be particularly associated with them: this is the making of thread and the weaving of garments.

The Reverend Kirk had this to say of the *sith* folk's skill:

> "Ther Women are said to Spine very fine, to Dy, to Tossue, and Embroyder: but whither it is as manuall Operation of substantiall refined Stuffs, with apt and solid Instruments, or only curious Cob-webs, impalpable Rainbows, and a fantastic Imitation of the Actions of more terrestricall Mortalls, since it transcended all the Senses of the Seere to discerne whither, I leave to conjecture as I found it."[201]

Quite a few other sources confirm the connection. Brownies performing household tasks will often undertake stages of the cloth making process, for instance dressing hemp (though at the same time their aversion to gifts of linen garments is to be recalled), carding wool and spinning tow (coarse hemp fibres used for ropes and the like). A mastery of cloth working is just one of the faery abilities that can be bestowed upon favoured mortals. In one case from Sutherland in the north of Scotland, a weaver who entered a faery knoll came away with an enchanted shuttle that helped him to weave three times as much cloth as anyone else. The fairies may also offer to help mortals whom they favour with teasing, carding, spinning, weaving and waulking, assistance that is generally well worth having because of the fairies' work rate. Even this may have a sting in the tail, though, either because it creates envy amongst neighbours who seek to interfere or because

---

201 Kirk, *Secret Commonwealth*, c.5.

the housewife becomes exhausted by the fairies' incessant demands for more work to do.[202]

Logically, of course, faeries have to be able to manufacture cloth and garments for themselves. Their royal courts and nobility are marked for their splendid robes and other costumes of green are central to many accounts. It is only really the dobbies who are habitually naked or dressed in rags. The northern faeries are said to spin with mountain flax, while the pixies of Cornwall use cotton-rush. Typical activities within the faery hills of Scotland include spinning and weaving. For example, there is an account from Skye of faeries heard 'waulking' (that is, fulling) some cloth and singing as they did so. At Green Hollow in Argyllshire there was reputed to be the site of a former cloth dying factory operated by the faeries of Lennox. When humans tried to steal the secrets of their natural plant dyes, it's said that the cloth workers concealed all their materials and fled. Those hidden dye-stuffs continue to stain the waters of a local pool. On the island of Coll, green silk produced by fairy workshops has been sighted, spread out to dry on a hillside at night.[203]

The *loireag* is a Highland faery specifically responsible for overseeing the making of cloth through all its stages, from loom to fulling. She was a stickler for the traditional methods and standards, apparently, and offerings of milk were made by home producers to propitiate her. Another Scottish spirit, the *gyre-carlin,* had comparable links to cloth-making. It was

---

202 J. G. Campbell, 'Black William the Piper'; MacGregor, *Peat Fire Flame,* Edinburgh: Moray Press,1937, 2; J. F. Campbell, *Popular Tales of the West Highlands,* vol.2, 62–3.

203 Addy, *Household Tales,* 135; R. Hawker, *Footprints of Former Men in Far Cornwall.* (London: John Lane, 1893); J. G. Campbell, *Superstitions of the Highlands and Islands,* 15 & 96; Evans Wentz, *Fairy Faith,* 98.

said that, if unspun flax was not removed from the distaff at the end of the year, she would steal it all. Conversely, if asked by a woman for the endowment of skill in spinning, she would enable the recipient to do three to four times as much work as other spinners. Like the *glaistig, gruagach* and *urisk,* the *loireag* expects to receive a libation of milk daily. If she doesn't receive her due, she'll simply suck it straight from the cattle, sheep and goats in the fields.[204]

The great productiveness of fairy spinners seems to be a very common theme across the whole British Isles. For example, a young Welsh woman from Garth Dorwen near Caernarfon used to go to spin with the *tylwyth teg* at night and she too reported on "the enormous amount of spinning [that] used to be done."[205]

We have extremely limited information about the actual quality of the fruits of fairy looms. Descriptions of fairy garments indicate that a range of cloths, from humble plaids and plain grey and brown materials, through to sumptuous satins, could be produced. Perhaps the best report is from the Scottish Lowlands: fairies entered a weaver's house one night to wash their child and accidentally left the baby's cap behind. The next day, the family found it and the in the weaver's professional eye judged it as a "very pretty article." He did not have long to study the item though, as the fairies retrieved it the following night.[206]

Thread and cloth making are not only marvellous, but according to faery tales, the process may also be perilous. On

---

204 Carmichael, *Carmina Gadelica,* vol.2, 320; E. Watson, 'Celtic Mythology,' *Celtic Review,* vol.5, 1908. 54.
205 Rhys, 214.
206 Campbell, 'The Lowland Fairies.'

the one hand, faeries may enter your home to carry out these tasks. In Scotland, it was believed to be the solitary female creatures – the *glaistig* and the *gyre-carlin* – who would most commonly enter human homes to spin, causing considerable disturbance and noise through the night. Such intrusions were not just a nuisance and a trespass – they risked too close a contact with these unpredictable beings, and measures had to be taken to prevent them. Several Manx tales warn how a failure to disengage the drive band on a spinning wheel before retiring to bed enables the faeries to come into a house overnight to use it for their own purposes. By inviting them in, albeit indirectly, you are potentially placing yourself in the power of the '*Li'l fellas.*' In the Scottish Highlands, this precaution was Christianised and it was said that the band should be disengaged on a Saturday night to prevent faery spinning early on a Sunday (Sabbath) morning.

Given the fairies' purported skills, it's curious that they so often seemed to resort to human homes to undertake the work, when you might anticipate them to have all the necessary equipment themselves. Nonetheless, if the drive bands are not slipped off spinning wheels, they will almost inevitably feel compelled to enter homes and use them whilst the human occupants are asleep. Trying to deny them access to the spinning wheel by disabling it will work, but it brings a risk too: if the fairies feel thwarted, they may cut a weaver's webs at night. Their presence can cause problems over and above the noise and chatter during the night, too. In one tale from Ross-shire, the fairies made use of a weaver's loom overnight, leaving in the morning a web of green cloth woven entirely from stolen wool. It seems that this was a very common trespass in human homes in the Highlands, to such an extent that a specific blessing is recorded to prevent gruagachs and fairy women interfering with looms (*"Bho gach gruagach is ban-sith"*).[207]

Equally puzzling are the strong views the fairies seem to hold about when it is appropriate for people to make thread. Evenings and Saturdays are particularly prohibited – at least on the Isle of Man. This may be evidence of some wider aversion, as baking in the evenings is also abhorred.[208]

Many fairy tales are founded upon the spinning of large amounts of thread by skilled and fast – working fairies. In one, a kindly faery woman named Habetrot (who's been called the patron spirit of spinning) appears and assists a daughter, along with a team of helpers including Scantlie Mab. In contrast, in the tale of *Tom-Tit-Trot* a girl has to spin a large quantity of yarn overnight or face beheading; the imp Tom-Tit-Trot helps her on condition that she will belong to him once the task has been completed – unless she can guess his name. Fortunately, she overhears it and is saved. *Sili-go-Dwt, Trwtyn-Tratyn, Terry-Top, Perrifool* and *Whuppity-Stoorie* are all similar British folk tales in which an elf helps with spinning and demands a forfeit unless its name is guessed. Many readers will spot the similarity of these stories to the Brothers Grimm's comparable tale of *Rumpelstiltskin*.[209]

Occasionally it's a faery who imposes the impossible spinning task. In one Scottish example a girl is abducted by the *sith* folk under a hillock and is told that she will be

---

207 Morrison, *Manx Fairy Tales*, 'Themselves'; Milne, *Myths & Superstitions of the Buchan District*, 17; Campbell, 'The lowland fairies;' J. F. Campbell, *Popular Tales*, 79; Carmichael, *Carmina Gadelica*, vol.1, 305.

208 Moore, *Folklore of the Isle of Man*, London: D. Nutt,1891, c.III; Joseph Train, *Historical Sketches*, Douglas: M. Quiggin, 1845, vol.2 c.XVIII.

209 Addy, *Household Tales*, 16 & 46.

held there until she has spun all the wool in a large sack and eaten all the meal in a huge chest. Despite her diligent efforts, neither diminish and she faces eternal confinement and labour until another captive soul tells her to rub spit on her left eyelid every morning. By so doing, she makes daily inroads into the wool and meal and finally escapes.[210]

These tales all stress the Good Folk's superior skills. The human characters are reliant upon their abilities, which border on the magical, and without which there may be fatal consequences. The spinning stories also strongly emphasise a dependent relationship between the faeries and humans. Perhaps too, there is some notion of exacting a high fee for the teaching of the faeries' remarkable craft knowledge.[211]

It's worth emphasising here the fact that the skills exercised by the faes are traditional individual 'cottage' crafts. They seem to lay great store by learning and experience. We hear stories of fairies being driven away by mills, or at least objecting strongly to them. Construction of a fulling mill on the Isle of Man drove the local fays into the mountains; when the mill at Kiondroghad on the Isle of Man was run overnight one time, the fays threw a broom at the millers in warning. Now, it's very probably fair to say that the main reasons in these two cases were flight from noise and disturbance and objection to their evening use of the mill being disturbed, but I wonder too if there might also be a hint of Luddite antipathy?[212]

One last story gives us an interesting and unexpected insight into fairy tailoring skills. A Welsh boy called Guto

---

210 Evans-Wentz *The Fairy Faith* 97; Rhys, *Celtic Folklore* 212; Scottish ballad *The Elfin Knight*.
211 see too chapter 19 of my *British Fairies*.
212 Waldron, *Isle of Man,* fn.56; Gill, *Second Manx Scrapbook,* c.III.

Bach ('Little Gruffydd') used to play with fairy children on the mountain near his home. One time he was gone with them for a very long time but came home with a suit of clothes, beautifully made for him from some material resembling white paper. His mother admired their workmanship, but burned them for fear of the *tylwyth teg* nonetheless.[213]

213 Jenkyn Thomas, *Welsh Fairy Book*, 'Guto Bach.'

Fairy Commerce

"Come buy our orchard fruits,
  Come buy, come buy."[214]

As already discussed; fairies buy and sell just like humans. One very common story that illustrates this concerns a fairy man who buys a horse. There are variants of detail, but the fay will always offer a fair price in gold and, generally, having concluded the bargain, he'll startle the seller by sinking into the earth along with his new mount.

MARKETS

Faery was believed in many respects to mirror human society: this extended to holding and frequenting fairs and markets. These occasions are not purely functional events intended for trade: witnesses have described the music that accompanies them and the fact that stalls will be decorated with garlands of flowers to enhance the beauty of the exquisitely crafted goods on display: "They have exposed their fairy Ware not to cheat but divert us." Dora Broome described a fairy fair on the Isle of Man that was rather

---

214 *Goblin Market,* Christina Rossetti.

different, nevertheless; it was full of delightful and tempting gifts and foods, but it was all an illusion created to catch a human being.[215]

Fairies are often presented as participating enthusiastically in commerce. Richard Bovet spoke to Somerset people in the 1680s and was told that the fairies "shewed themselves in great Companies at divers times; at some times they would seem to dance, at other times to keep a great Fair or Market." He enquired about this and was told of the famous fairy fair on the Blackdown Hills, held in the summertime, which featured pewterers, pedlars and fruit and ale sellers. Human buyers tended to steer clear of these events, though, as "everyone that had [attended] had received great damage by it."[216] Other well-known fairs were held by the pixies near St Just, Paul, Breage and at St Germoe in Cornwall.[217]

If one is polite and respectful, it is even possible for humans to trade with the fairies at their own markets. This amenability to a human presence is rare though – normally the intrusion is resented and, at the very least, the fair will vanish as soon as the mortal presence is detected; at worst, those intruding may be jostled and even lamed. Ruth Tongue heard such an account in Somerset, the most interesting aspect of which is that change given in dry leaves became gold and silver at home the next day – contrary to the normal nature of fairy 'gold'; more typical is the story

---

215 G. Berkeley, *Alaphron*, II, VII, xxv, 190; Broome, *More Fairy Tales*, 8–15.

216 Bovet, *Pandaemonium*, London: J. Walthoe, 1684, 207; Keightley, *Fairy Mythology*, 294–5.

217 Blight, *A Week at Land's End*, Truro: Lake and Lake, 1876, 195; Evans Wentz, 171.

told of innkeepers being paid in coins which turned out to be pieces of horn or leather.[218]

Besides holding their own, fairies will also attend human markets and fairs. In many respects, this is welcome. It's said in Wales that their presence gives a buzz to markets and makes the business brisk and that the fairies' chatter at night always peaked when the prices were high at Llangefni market. When the *tylwyth teg* were present at Bala market, they would swell the noise in the market place, something that was taken as a sure sign that prices would rise. At Cardigan market it was said that if the corn prices went up, yet all the grain was sold by the end of the day despite this, it was confirmation that the *Plant Rhys Ddwfn* had been in attendance. Sometimes, of course, this known link made the market traders greedy and they would put up their prices on the assumption that the *tylwyth teg* would buy anyway: this effrontery and over confidence might lead to the market being deserted – as happened at Fishguard, which lost out to Haverfordwest. Sometimes the fairies would be visible: "some very strange people were wont to be seen" at Fishguard for example; in other places they were present but unseen. If visible, as at Laugharne and Milford Haven, they did their business very formally, putting down the exact money without needing to ask the price and then going on their way. In some places, such as Cardigan, it was believed that human factors did the purchasing on the fairies' behalf. At other times, perhaps predictably, the fairies used their magical powers to get goods without the necessity of

---

218 Tregarthen, 'Pobel Vean Fair,' (1906), *Folklore Tales; County Folklore – Somerset,* vol.8, 112; Heywood, *The Hierarchie of Blessed Angels.*

payment. A very common theme in fairy lore is the midwife who unintentionally touches an eye with ointment that dispels fairy glamour so she can see fairies stealing goods at a market or fair. Whether she simply greets the fae or cries 'stop thief,' she's blinded.[219] In the fairy scheme of things, the primary offence that has occurred in these cases is that of a human stealing the gift of second sight, to which they are not entitled and from which they shall derive no pleasure or benefit. This theft deserves punishment; the fairies' own pilfering in comparison is negligible.[220]

An interesting variant upon the midwife plot comes from the island of Guernsey. There, a nurse was fetched to tend a sick fairy child inside the burial chamber called *Le Creux es Faies*. The nurse believed herself to be in richly furnished rooms until the baby spat in her eye, upon which she saw she was really in a cave. She kept quiet about this and stayed until the child was well. Later, though, she spotted a fairy shoplifting in town. She challenged him, in response to which he too spat in her eye – and she lost her sight. A Welsh variant of this theme involves two farm servants on Anglesey who were woken in the night by two fairy men, asking them to wash and dress their babies. The girls did as they were bidden and were well paid for it, but a decade later one girl saw one of the two men stealing money from a shop in Caergybi. He pulled out her left eye in response. A less violent version of the same episode involves the fairies leaving behind some "stuff" after washing their babies at

---

219 Owen, *Welsh Folklore,* 108; Evans Wentz 139; Rhys 99, 147, 159, 160, 161, 167, 198 & 213.
220 E. Tregarthen, 'The Nurse Who Broke Her Promise,' 1940, in *Folklore Tales,* 2020.

night. A servant girl rubs an itch on her eye after handling the substance and later is able to see a fairy stealing cakes at Llanrwst fair. He merely rubs her eye to deprive her of the second sight.[221]

In the case of Christina Rossetti's *Goblin Market*, its purpose was not commerce but as a means of luring in innocent humans. It's a literary confounding of two authentic themes – fairy trade and the perils of fairy food. In the poem, Jeanie had tasted the goblins' fruits and thereafter:

> "pined and pined away
> Sought them by night and day,
> Found them no more but dwindled and grew grey."

Some folk tales certainly indicate that fairies possess their own independent wealth, in the form of gold, silver and cattle, though it must be conceded that this may originally have been stolen from humans, as pilfering was consistently reported to be a key element in the elvish economy.[222] Fairies are, therefore, known to pay quite properly for items and services rendered. In one story they feed a pregnant sow and, when she has farrowed, take the piglets but leave money in their place.[223] An odd account from Wales records the fairly common practice of fairies leaving gold in return for water left out by humans – except in this case the coins were said to be

---

221 MacCulloch, *Guernsey Folklore,* London: Elliott Stock, 1903, 208; W. Cobb, 'Anglesey Folklore, from Near Holyhead,' *Y Cymmrodor*, 1886, vol.7, 197; 'City & Country Chit-Chat,' *North Wales Chronicle & Advertiser,* July 19th 1884, 4.
222 Evans Wentz 106, 144, 147 & 151.
223 *A Pleasant Treatise of Witches,* 1634.

of unknown provenance, not British currency but unfamiliar pieces marked with a harp on one side.[224]

Around Bangor it was said that the *tylwyth teg* "have plenty of money at their command, which they could bestow on people whom they liked."[225] With this wealth, they would reward those whose behaviour gained their favour (see earlier). Something very much similar was said of the trows on Shetland. They are reported to have plenty of gold and silver; however, this boundless wealth is also described as ephemeral. They seldom give it away and, even when they do, the recipient is always disappointed.[226]

A further curious detail concerning the commercial and capitalist nature of faery comes from the *Robin Goodfellow, his mad pranks and merry jests,* in which we are informed that the fairies would lend money to the poor to assist them – and this without interest:

"For the use demand we nought,
   Our own is all we desire."[227]

This sounds like some sort of social finance, but if they did not pay on the due date, the borrowers would be pinched or punished "in their goods, so that they never thrive 'til they have paid us."

Interestingly, the fairy interest in commerce seems to extend to some humans as well, judging by the evidence of

---

224 John Rhys, *Celtic Folklore* 6.
225 Evans Wentz 142.
226 'Manners, Traditions & Superstitions of the Shetlanders,' *Fraser's Magazine,* vol.34, 1846, 485; 'Shetland Folklore,' *Glasgow Herald,* April 9th 1886, 10.
227 *The Pranks of Puck.*

one case from Gower, in Wales. A man called Will was on his way to Swansea market early one morning when he came across some fairies dancing. They encouraged him to join them and, after participating for quite a time, he was allowed to continue his journey. The fairies declared, "Will dance well; the last going to market and the first that shall sell." Sure enough, although he arrived very late in Swansea that day, he was the first to make a sale.[228]

FAIRY DEPENDENCE

Despite all this evidence of a separate fairy economy, there was also a constant theme in folklore of the fair folk being to some degree dependent upon humans for the provision of basic items. Frequently, they might rely upon people to provide them with heated water for bathing; as we have already seen as well, they also seem to lack various basic domestic items and skills to satisfy which they have to resort to human aid. For example, a broken plough or baking 'peel' will have to be repaired by a man and the fairies have regularly borrowed kitchen gear from their mortal neighbours. Recompense in the form of food was generally made.[229]

In summary, one's assessment of the balance of the faery economy between booty and barter in large measure will depend upon whether or not you regard them as primarily malign or benign. For earlier generations, it will be obvious that the concept of thieving fairies provided a ready explanation of poor harvests, declining yields and lost or

---

228 Evans-Wentz, *Fairy Faith*, 160.
229 Rhys 63, 220, 221, 227, 228, 229 & 241.

mislaid items. Our 'good neighbours', meanwhile, might be expected to prefer pilfering to purchasing as it involved a great deal less effort to live on the fruits of others' labours; moreover, they were considerably aided in their larceny by their ability to disappear. One final consideration obtrudes itself: according to John Rhys, fairies can only count to five, the total fingers on one hand. This greatly limited their numerical skills, plainly, and might incline one more to the belief that theft would be preferred to honest trade...[230]

---

230 *Celtic Folklore* c.VII.

Traffic with the Good Neighbours

As already indicated, there is a variety of ways in which humans can enter into commercial arrangements with the fairies, under which exchanges of goods, labour and money are made. There are more forms of transaction to be described, but before this is done it is worthwhile stressing that all such traffic brings risks for the human partners. Not only is there the risk of being cheated or outwitted by the fays; there is also the ever-present danger involved with any close contact with the supernatural. Any kind of sojourn in Faery, or the consumption of fairy foodstuffs, is perilous for the physical and psychological health of the individual. For example, a man from the Braes of Portree, in the Isle of Skye, had an arrangement with the local fairies whereby they undertook to sow and to harvest his crops. They did this promptly and efficiently, but all his family grew up "peculiar in their minds," it was said.[231]

---

231 Campbell, *Superstitions,* 99.

GIFTS TO FAERIES

One way of keeping on the right side of the Good Folk is to make gifts to them. This shows respect and, hopefully, encourages their favour. As noted earlier, the colliers in North Derbyshire used to leave one hundred weight of coal in the mine each week as an offering, doubtless hoping that faery favour would sustain rich seams and prevent pit collapses. The Dartmoor pixies always appreciate a gift of pins or ribbon left at the Pixies' Cave on Sheepstor and will reward the donor.[232]

There seems to be a very fine line, though, between gifts made out of respect and something less voluntary. Sometimes we seem to be dealing with a sacrifice to an angry deity. One Dartmoor sheep farmer's flock was plagued by disease; he concluded that the only remedy was to go to the top of a tor and slaughter a sheep to the pixies – a move which promptly alleviated the problem. A contemporary example comes from a school child in Highland Scotland: he'd knocked down some toadstools and, as these might have been a faery's 'wee house', he placed some money under his pillow for the Tooth Faery to take, in order to say sorry. There's a good deal of confusion here between old and new ideas: the Tooth Faery seems to have been chosen as a familiar and friendly representative of fairykind generally and as one who's in the habit of entering into deals with children. In this case, however, she's being given coins instead of leaving them in exchange for milk teeth, a reversal of her conventionally recognised role. Although this child's understanding of the function of the Tooth Faery was unusual, he had nonetheless fully grasped the fundamental

---

232 Addy *Household Tales*.141; Coxhead, *Devon Traditions,* 50.

dynamic of the human relationship with supernaturals – they are a dangerous people who should be propitiated, so something is offered to them in the hope of forgiveness and future goodwill.[233]

On other occasions, people's 'gifts' to the Good Folk bear a closer resemblance to a protection racket. Faery lore expert Katharine Briggs noted that the Good Folk can be "arrant thieves" and that making offerings to them is a way of deflecting their mischief and displeasure. She described it as a form of blackmail and there definitely seems to be some truth in this. For example, on the Isle of Arran, it was the practice always to leave the fairies a share of the corn dried in a kiln. To fail to leave this 'tithe' was sure to bring bad luck to the farmer – and it might well be imagined that this misfortune could take the form of crop failure or a fire in the kiln.[234]

There is one special class of offerings that deserves particular attention. This is the practice of making donations, or gifts, of clothing to fays. We find these being made usually to brownies, but boggarts, hobs and even banshees have also been offered clothes. It's a problematic area because of the varied and unpredictable reaction of the faery to the items presented. One thing is for sure: that the faeries can be very touchy on the subject. At Upleatham, near Redcar, the hob attached to the Oughtred family was outraged by the mere sight of a workman's jacket mistakenly left hanging overnight on a winnowing machine in the barn.[235]

---

233 V. C. Clinton-Baddeley, *Dartmoor*, 1925, 97; Bennett in Narvaez *Good People*, Lexington: University of Kentucky Press,1997,11 1–112.
234 Briggs, "English Fairies" 274; MacKenzie, *Book of Arran*, 270.
235 Richard Blakeborough, *Wit, Character, Folklore & Customs of the North Riding of Yorkshire*: (London: Henry Frowde, 1898), 203.

Some faeries accept clothes with delight; some are deeply offended by the idea of wearing human garments. In either instance, though, the outcome seems to be exactly the same: whether the faeries put on the clothes or reject them, they will depart from the service of the family or house for whom they had previously toiled so devotedly. An example of this comes from the Scottish Highlands. One family had a spirit called a *caointeach* (keener) attached to it; she would wail and moan before any death. One wet, cold and windy night she was heard outside a house in which a family member lay ill. One of the company present put a plaid outside and called to the *caointeach* to put on the tartan and move herself to the side of the house sheltered from the gale. She was never heard to mourn again.[236]

There seems to be a variety of reasons why clothing can alienate faeries. One story about the Manx brownie, the fynoderee, reveals that the offence can arise from the fact that wearing our clothes will make him ill, causing aches in head and feet. In other cases, it appears to be the mere gift itself, as in the case of a brownie at Boghall Farm, Dollar, who was offended by blankets and departed, taking all the farm's good fortune with him. In contrast, some fays appear to want clothes (and even ask directly for clothing in recompense for their labours) but they may still be upset by the quality of what they're given – in most cases finding garments of coarse hemp or linen unacceptable (because presumably they

---

236 Roberts *Folklore of Yorkshire*, 97; Taylor & Troon, *Midlothian Folk Tales*, Stroud: History Press, 2018, 112; L. Spence *The Fairy Tradition in Britain* (London: Rider & Co,1948) 36–37; MacDougall *Folk Tales*, 215.

wanted cotton or wool). Once again, the perceived insult will lead to their prompt departure.[237]

Sometimes humans get it wrong and give the wrong sort of clothes. In other cases, a gift is wanted – but it isn't garments. This set out for us in a ballad, the *Life of Robin Goodfellow*, published in 1628. In response to being presented with a linen waistcoat, Robin exclaims:

> "Because thou lay'st me himpen, hampen,
> I will neither bolt nor stampen.
> 'Tis not your garments new or old,
> That Robin loves; I feele no cold.
> Had you left me milke or creame,
> You should have had a pleasing dreame;
> Because you left no drop nor crum,
> Robin never more will come."

The faeries in all these cases have undertaken voluntarily to attach themselves to a household and to work there without acknowledgement or substantial reward (other than the classic bowl of milk or cream – and this sharing of food might be seen as accepting the brownie as part of the household and not as a mere worker). Providing payment in kind seems to violate this unspoken arrangement and to seek to formalise it on quasi-contractual grounds. Food left out at night doesn't seem to create the same bond or obligation as that which arises from providing clothes made specially. There may be a connotation of servant's livery or uniform here, too –

---

237 Spence *The Fairy Tradition in Britain* 36–37; *County Folklore*, vol.7, 317; I. Barton, *North Yorkshire Folk Tales* (Stroud, The History Press, 2014) 3; Roberts, *Folklore of Yorkshire*, 96–98.

of the brownie's subjugation to control and organisation of the human household. Perhaps, as well, as these fays tend to choose to go about naked or dressed in tatters, the offer of human clothes may be offensive because it represents another aspect of subjection to human society and behaviour.[238]

There is one anomalous account from Dartmoor of coins being left out for the pixies at night. This case notwithstanding, paying for the work to be done by the fays is not how this relationship functions and to attempt to commercialise it will virtually always prove to be a bad idea.[239]

FAIRIES AS DOMESTIC SERVANTS

I mentioned earlier that human captives are often taken into fairyland to act as slaves. Conversely, and rather surprisingly, some fairies seem happy to undertake chores for humans, whether that be strenuous physical tasks or finishing off household jobs that haven't been completed?

We are already familiar with the activities of the brownie and related faery species (boggarts, broonies, *gruagachs* and *glaistigs*) who will attach themselves to a particular family, estate or farmstead and perform a variety of agricultural and domestic functions under a relationship that may be regarded as some sort of contract for service, with the fairy being accepted as having a clear role and place within the

---

238 J. Bailey, *Lancashire Folk Tales*, Stroud, The History Press, 2014, 91; Couch, *History of Polperro*, 136; HGT, 'Pixies or Pisgies', *Notes & Queries*, 1850, no.61, 511; R. Pearse Chope, 'Folklore of Devon', in *London Devonian Yearbook*, 1910, 112.

239 Crossing, *Tales of Dartmoor Pixies*, c.3.

household. In return for the work done, food, drink and, often an allocated time to enjoy the shelter and warmth of the humans' home are granted. The faery has a recognised position within the wider clan or 'familia'.

In this section, I'm rather more interested in the cases where the fairies appear to do odd-jobs for humans. Remuneration may be provided, but there isn't the long-term relationship that is usually understood to exist with the brownies and boggarts. These arrangements can take a number of forms. There are the cases where the fairy comes to the human home to do the work. On Guernsey, it was said that the fairies would help industrious individuals. If an unfinished piece of knitting, such as a stocking, was left on the hearth or by the oven along with a bowl of porridge, by morning the work would be done and the bowl would be empty. However, if the reason that the task was unfinished was the person's idleness, the faery response would be to deal out some blows instead. On the island of Jersey it was reported that if servants left out unfinished work (such as needlework) with a piece of cake, the fairies would complete it overnight – and do much of the next day's work too. On the British mainland, in Staffordshire, the tradition was the same: small household tasks would be carried out in return for gifts of food or tobacco. In Devon, the pixies were reported to enter houses at night by the keyholes. They would then do the cleaning, or complete the brewing, so long as bread and milk or water, towels and soap were left out for them.[240]

Comparable to these last examples is information from the Scottish Highlands to the effect that a girl's fairy lover, who

---

240 MacCulloch, *Guernsey Folklore*, 203; *Folklore* vol.25, 1914, 245; W. Witcutt, 'Notes on Staffordshire Folklore', *Folklore* vol.53, 1942, 89; F. Hancock, *The Parish of Selworthy*, 1877, 247.

lived near her home in a fairy hill, would help her out with her daily chores, such as cutting peat turfs for the fire. Of course, the motivation here was love, which may well distinguish it from the cases already described.[241]

Somewhat at odds with most of the foregoing is a case in which a man's laziness was encouraged by the fairies doing all his work for him at night. A miller of Mulinfenachan, called Strong Malcolm, used to put everything ready in his mill before he went to bed, knowing that all the grinding would be done by morning. If straw needed to be threshed for the cattle, or grain winnowed, these jobs would be done if tools and raw materials were left out. Anyone who tried to spy on the activities would be forcibly expelled.

None of this was done out of kindness though. When another mill burned down locally, the fairies were heard to exclaim "We will have plenty of meal now… and Strong Malcolm must henceforth work for himself or starve." The explanation of this account rests on two points. One is that food stuffs lost by fire (or perhaps just dropped on the ground) went to the fairies as their rightful property. Secondly, it will be apparent that they had been taking a 'commission' for the work that they did for Malcolm. They had been keeping a share of all the flour, grain and such like – and with the fire, they no longer had to work for this. Although the Guernsey fairies objected to laziness, those of Duthil in Inverness-shire didn't mind – because it was profitable for them not to do so.[242]

---

241 Mrs Grant, *Essays on the Superstitions of the Highlanders of Scotland*, 1811, 285.

242 MacDougall & Calder, *Folk Tales and Fairy Lore*, 187.

LOANS TO THE FAIRIES

There are regular transactions between fairies and humans in the form of requests for loans from the former. Sometimes the items in question are large and expensive pieces of equipment that will only rarely be required – carts and teams of horses required for moving house are a very good example. It's understandable why anyone might avoid the outlay of maintaining something that will only be used every few years – or even more infrequently. For example, when the pixies residing on a farm at Withypool on Exmoor decided to move to the other side of Winsford Hill, a distance of around four to five miles, in order to escape the sound of the local church bells, they begged use of the farmer's cart and horses. Such equipment might be needed much more regularly, all the same. On Guernsey the Garis family was visited nightly by their fairy neighbours, asking for the loan of their farm cart until dawn. This regular inconvenience was offset by the fact that fairies always promised to return the wagon in perfect condition, with any damage to the woodwork repaired with silver.[243]

As the Guernsey example starts to suggest, despite the apparent strength of the fairy economy, with markets, agriculture and manufacture, fairies are still often portrayed in folklore accounts as dependent for many basic items of food or equipment upon their human neighbours. Shortage of provisions may reflect fluctuations in the availability of homegrown produce, but the seeming lack of basic utensils is more puzzling. The regular loans may indicate material

---

243 Edgar MacCulloch, *Guernsey Folklore,* 1903, 212.

poverty, but part of the purpose of loans may be to establish a relationship of reciprocity between the two parties, which may then lead to other requests. In one case, a very grand 'fairy queen' dressed in green came begging for oatmeal, something she repaid with the very best quality meal at the promised time. It seems, though, that this may have been a preliminary to asking to use the lender's water mill for grinding the fairy corn. Something similar happened to a cottager living at Airlie in Angus-shire. She was visited by a mysterious old woman asking to borrow salt one day, although the cottage stood alone with no neighbouring homes in sight. The little woman regularly visited after that, borrowing and lending a variety of small articles and then disappearing behind a tree outside. Eventually, the housewife was outside the cottage one day pouring away the household waste when the *sith* woman appeared again – but this time to ask her to tip her water elsewhere as it presently was running into the hollow by the tree where she lived. A very similar story was told on the Isle of Man, in which the relationship and obligations established through a loan of meal – and its repayment with an inexhaustible supply of flour wrapped in a cloth – culminated in a request that the farmer change around the way his cows were stabled in the byre, putting their troughs where their tails had been and so preventing their waste running down into the fairies' home beneath.[244]

As just seen in the Airlie case, a regular feature of these experiences is the sudden and unexplained appearance of the fairy borrower. This reflects the invisible or hidden nature of most fairy homes. The fae might suddenly vanish into the air

---

244 J. F. Campbell, *Popular Tales*, 66; *Legends of Scottish Superstition*, Edinburgh: W. & H. Robinson, 1848, 30–32; Roeder, *Manx Folktales*, 15.

or disappear into an unlikely location, such as a lake or a tree. Whatever their reasons, fairies will frequently enter human homes seeking a loan. Amongst the items borrowed have been salt, griddles, kettles, flour and oatmeal. Besides pure good neighbourliness, why should humans comply? There are several very sound reasons.

Firstly, there is pure self-interest, in that not only are these loans returned, but they are always repaid, often several-fold and sometimes with better quality goods. For instance, oatmeal might be replaced with barley meal and the meal returned might prove to be inexhaustible. A woman at Glasserton in south west Scotland was approached by a small woman asking for a little milk. She readily complied and was promised never to be without a pinch of snuff thereafter – but, as it turned out, this also meant a plentiful supply of milk and corn.[245]

As with all fairy gifts, these should never be rejected nor looked at askance. A Kirkcudbrightshire family lent oatmeal to a fairy and received meal back in due course. Everyone in the household was happy to eat this fairy food, except for one boy who worked as a farmhand – and he died shortly afterwards. This case suggests that much of the lending to fairies is undertaken not out of a spirit of generosity, but in fear of the consequences of refusing a loan.[246]

The recompense received later may be especially great if the person who lends is themselves deprived or inconvenienced in some way. A faery woman visited a Highland home and asked for a cup of flour. Even though supplies were low, as it was nearly time for the new harvest, the housewife gave

245 Wood, *Witchcraft & Superstitious Record*, 165.
246 J. F. Campbell, *Popular Tales*, 66; Campbell, *Superstitions*, 150 & 151; Sutherland, *Folklore Gleanings*, 23.

her visitor what she asked for – and in return was granted a never-ending supply of meal. The person who refuses to lend, particularly where they are very capable of helping, will end up with nothing.[247]

Another motivation for loaning, undoubtedly, is what the result of refusal may be. A woman in Sutherland was visited by a fairy woman asking for the loan of a 'lippie' of meal (a lippie is a measure of dry goods like grain, and is one quarter of a peck). Just as the housewife was about to hand some over, they both noticed that the corn drying kiln on the nearby hillside was ablaze. The *sith* woman immediately told her the loan was no longer necessary, for she would soon have plenty of her own (because what was destroyed in the blaze would come to her. Whether or not the fire was deliberate is not clear).[248]

In poor agricultural communities where food is in short supply and assets are limited, there may be understandable reluctance to part with goods, even for a short time. One resolution to this was tried by a woman on Sanntraigh. She had a very useful kettle (cooking pot) and a *sith* woman used to visit regularly to borrow it. She wouldn't speak, but would simply walk in and take the item. The housewife, in response, would say:

"A smith is able to make,
  Cold iron hot with coal.
  The due of a kettle is bones,
  And to bring it back again whole."

---

247 Anon, *Folklore and legends: Scotland,* W. W. Gibbings, 1889, 98; Murray, *Scottish Gaelic Texts,* Edinburgh: Scottish Gaelic Texts Society, 2009, vol.7, no's. 70 & 169.
248 J. F. Campbell, *Popular Tales,* 71.

The *sith* woman would always return the kettle the next day, full of flesh and bones. This arrangement continued happily for a long time, until one day the wife had to go away for a day and left her husband at home. He was told what to say when the fairy visitor arrived, but in the event, he panicked and locked the door against her. The *sith* woman had the pot anyway, making it fly out of the smoke hole in the roof.

When the woman returned home, she was dismayed to hear what her husband had done. Angrily the housewife went to the nearby knoll to recover her cooking pot. The door was open and she walked in and picked it up, full of the remains of the faes' last meal. They set the dogs on her though, and whilst she managed to get home uninjured, she had to tip out all the contents along the way to distract the hounds. The *sith* woman never came borrowing after that day and the family lost its supply of free meat.[249]

As this story demonstrates, the fairies can be peremptory and intrusive, simply walking into houses unannounced and uninvited and helping themselves. In one Scottish story a housewife was troubled by faery women suddenly appearing at her cottage asking to borrow items or, unbidden, undertaking household tasks for her, such as spinning wool into thread. This became very tiresome and, on advice from a local wise man, the decision was made to demolish the house and rebuild it elsewhere.[250]

---

249 J. F. Campbell, *Popular Tales*, no.52; McPhail, 'Folklore from the Hebrides II,' *Folklore* vol.8, 381, has a version in which a slightly different charm is used and in which the housewife is savaged by the dogs and dies whilst rescuing her kettle; see too Campbell, *Superstitions*, 57.

250 J. G. Campbell, *Waifs & Strays of Celtic Tradition*. London: Nutt, 1895, vol.5, (Argyllshire Series), 83–86.

Removing yourself from the faes is probably the best course of action: in one Welsh case a woman lost her temper with faes who kept coming to her house to borrow kitchen implements. She demanded that they grant her two wishes in return for the item they wanted. She asked that, when she awoke, the first item she touched would break (she wanted to get rid of a projecting stone in her wall) and that the second would lengthen (she wanted to extend a roll of cloth she had). The faeries gave her exactly what she'd asked for – but the wishes didn't come true as the woman had planned: the next morning the first thing she touched was her ankle, the second her nose.[251]

It was the opinion in Caithness, in the north of Scotland, that the fairies were very poor people with whom to have such dealings. An old woman, called Bell the Bride, who was a renowned fairy expert, told a late Victorian folklorist that you should never lend scissors and other such implements to the fairies because "some of them were na' honest an' would na' gie 'em back." The worst offender of all, seemingly, was called One Eye, "a lang, lanky chiel wi' ae ee in the middle of his broo" who never returned anything. You have been warned.[252]

LOANS FROM FAERIES

The faeries constantly seek loans from humans. They will also make loans in the other direction, but these are very rare indeed. In the Airlie case mentioned earlier, a familiar

---

251 Jenkyn Thomas, *Welsh Fairy Book,* 'A Fairy Borrowing.'
252 Polson, in Horne, *The County of Caithness,* Wick: W. Rae, 1907, 107.

pattern of mutual loans seems to have developed. The only instance in which fairies habitually lent to humans was that of the Frensham cauldron, described by John Aubrey. Within the parish was Borough Hill, on which lay a stone about two metres in length. If a person knocked on the stone and stated what they needed to borrow and when it would be handed back, they would be told by a voice when to return, at which time the item requested, whether it was money or a yoke of oxen, would be there for them. Ultimately a borrower asked for a large cooking pot but failed to restore it on the appointed day and the fairies refused to take it back and answered no more requests for assistance. The pot ended up in the church and was seen there by Aubrey, although it has disappeared since.[253]

In a story from the Highlands of Scotland, it's said that the man who first borrowed a quern from the fairies never returned it and, in revenge, they took all the benefit (*toradh*) from the crops of his farm for the following year. The fairies also seem to be very exact about *what* should be repaid. An Islay man had been loaned oatmeal by the fairies and, in expression of his gratitude, he returned over-measure to them. They were offended by this and never made loans to him again.[254]

FAERY FILCHING

Of course, if you won't give or lend to the faes, they'll probably get whatever they want anyway. The fairies steal from humans; it is one of their defining characteristics. This thievery can be

253 Aubrey, *Natural History of Surrey,* 1718, vol.3, 366.
254 Campbell, *Superstitions,* 150 & 151.

in the form of steady depredations of farm produce like grain or milk, the taking of a whole beast at once or theft of goods for sale from shops and from stalls at markets and fairs. Needless to say, this larceny is intended to go unnoticed by humankind and a very common theme in fairy lore is the midwife who has accidentally given herself the second sight – until she spots a fairy stealing in a market place – for which she's blinded.[255] A variant upon this comes from the Herefordshire town of Kington. A local girl was abducted by dancing fairies, but she was rescued from the ring a year and a day later. Back in the human world, she found a job in the town. Whilst absent in the fairy dance, she had acquired the second sight and very soon realised that the fairies were entering and stealing from the shop where she now worked. She warned her employer what was happening, but also managed to let the fairies know that they had been discovered, without disclosing that she could see their larcenies.[256]

The faes will take anything that has been lost, destroyed, discarded or rejected by humans; they've been described as "thieves by inclination" – habitual criminals, if you will... For example, liquids that are spilled and crumbs of food dropped during cooking or eating go to the faeries, as do goods that are destroyed by fire and cattle that have died. It was thought in the Highlands that when a cow fell off a cliff, the only way to stop the fays taking the carcase was to act quickly and put a nail in it.[257]

255 J. Couch, *History of Polperro*, 1871, 138.

256 Rhys 99, 198 & 213; E. Leather, *Folklore of Herefordshire,* Hereford: Jakeman & Carver, 1912, 45.

257 Lewes, *Stranger Than Fiction*, London: Rider & Son, 1911, 160; Grant Stewart, *Popular Superstitions*, 122–124; MacGregor, *Peat Fire Flame* 3.

As well as asserting a right to wasted items, the faeries seem to claim some sort of tax or tithe on the rest of our goods. A woman who gleaned too thoroughly in the fields after harvest was roughly handled by the faeries because she had deprived them of what they regarded as their customary share of the grain (the same consideration may well lie behind the practice of leaving some apples in an orchard at harvest time, as mentioned before). Undoubtedly related to this is the Cornish idea that to ensure a good harvest the reapers should always throw a piece of bread over their shoulder and spill a few drops of their beer at meal break. A Cornish tin miner called Tom Trevorrow, who never left a crumb of his lunch for the knockers in the mine, lost all his luck because of his meanness. These ideas seem to be somewhere between an offering and an indication of the faeries' sense that they're entitled to a share of all the goods and food that we produce.[258]

This attitude of entitlement easily shades into out and out theft by the Good Folk. There appears to be little compunction about this and the nocturnal household invasions described earlier will often be for more than just playing pranks. I've already mentioned the faeries' notorious habit of stealing milk and cream. Other goods and foodstuffs are equally vulnerable. Northamptonshire poet John Clare recorded the popular sentiment on this: mice were not reckoned greater thieves, he wrote, and the faeries were compared to wasps in a grocer's shop, streaming in through the keyholes, 'pop, pop, pop.'[259]

Food is the most commonly stolen item across Britain, but the faeries have even been known to take cooking implements.

258 Murray, *Tales from Highland Perthshire*, no.103.
259 John Clare, *January*.

In the Highlands, it used to be the case that hand mills were particularly vulnerable to theft. The way to protect them was always to turn the grind stones sun-wise during use. The trows of Shetland will even steal fire from a human hearth if their own goes out.

The faeries will steal from anywhere, too. Cattle in fields are vulnerable, homes will be entered and they are confident enough to enter shops and markets and steal openly there. For example, from the English Lake District we have an account of faeries mingling with the crowds at Ambleside market. When they found an item they wanted, they blew in the eyes of the stall-holders, rendering themselves invisible, and then made off with the goods.[260]

Mostly, fairies' thefts are larceny, rather than robbery – that is, without the use of violence. This is not always the case. A pedlar called Scobie, of Bridge-hill of Kilbryde near Dunblane, did regular business with the fairies and was known in the district for always having strange gold coins, which people assumed to be fairy currency. One evening he had been visiting a friend and prepared to leave after dark. The friend felt the pedlar looked 'fay-like' (as if something magical was about to happen) and offered to escort him home. Scobie refused, despite hearing some odd noises outside, and set off alone. He never reached his home. A warlock was consulted on the disappearance; he went into a trance before declaring that the man had been pulled into a fairy hill. He warned: 'they'll squeeze his innards out, steal his goods and spew him out.' Sure enough, after further searching, his body was found but his pack was never seen again.[261]

---

260 Cowper, *Hawkshead,* London: Bemrose & Sons, 1899, 307.
261 Monteath, *Dunblane Traditions,* Glasgow: John Miller, 1887, 55.

Curiously, whilst the faeries show no qualms over taking human property, it is forbidden for them to steal off each other. The story is told on Shetland of a trow boy who was often seen wandering alone and miserable. Apparently, he had stolen a silver spoon from another trow and his punishment was to be banished from beneath the hills. It seems that faeries can be strict about how they should treat each other, as well as how humans should behave towards them, yet they can be blissfully amoral in their treatment of us.[262]

Another irony is that, whilst the faeries don't hesitate to steal, they don't like to be unjustly accused of theft. A man called Rob o' t' Deans who lived at Walsden in West Yorkshire was very prone to thieving off his neighbours, but he would always seem very concerned over their losses, helped to search for the missing items – and would loudly blame the faeries. The fays took note of his calumnies and, eventually, they got their revenge. He was crossing the moor one night, carrying home some stolen cloth, when he came upon a faery dance. He sneaked up and watched it for hours, eventually falling asleep where he was hidden. The faeries knew all about his presence, of course, and Rob stayed fast asleep until the next morning when early risers discovered him, still holding the stolen bolts of worsted.[263]

---

262 Saxby, *Shetland Traditional Lore*, Edinburgh: Grant & Murray, 1932, 140.
263 Billingsley, *West Yorkshire Folk Tales*, Stroud: The History Press, 2010, 156.

Fairy Frauds

As I have described, the fairies will sometimes defraud humans, striking bargains with them and settling these in coins that turns out later to be leaves, mushrooms or pebbles. Perhaps this is pure theft on the fairies' part, or perhaps it is a calculating exploitation of the weakness that we humans have for gold. The fairy world can often seem less material than our own and, in their use of rubbish as currency; perhaps our neighbours mock our obsessions with gain and possessions.

In truth, though, the main frauds linked to fairies are those imposed upon humans by other humans, by taking advantage of others' belief. These were cynical exploitations of others' gullibility, but the popular view of Faery could in fact be so jaundiced that there was not even thought to be honour amongst thieves. In the ballad, *A Monstrous Shape*, published in 1639, Robin Goodfellow is portrayed as a servant of the fairy queen – and being cheated by her, for she:

> "chang'd him like a Fairie elfe;
> For all his money, goods and pelfe,
> She gull'd him."

SIMPLE MINDED FAITH?

The cynical say that there is no such thing as Faerie. It follows from this that those who believe otherwise are often regarded as fools and simpletons – and are treated as such, not only being mocked but exploited. Faerie can then provides both the mechanism for fraud as well as the means of the crime's concealment: for who is likely to confess to his neighbours that he has spent his hard-won wealth on such an illusory prospect as a meeting with a person who doesn't exist?

Nevertheless, history shows us that there are those desperate enough to meet with faeries as to risk money and reputation and those who are ready and willing to deprive them of both. In 1630 William Vaughan set out an *Arraignment of slander, perjury, blasphemy and other malicious sinnes*. In it he exposed how:

> "Our common witchcraft, soothsaying, consultations with spirits and conjurations are nothing but cousenages, leger-de-mains, impostures, confederacy or cony-catching in making folks believe that they can prophesy, work miracles, tell fortunes, reveal stolen goods, heal sicknesses and griefs with charming runes; yea, these seducing spirits aver that they walk every week with the Fayries, that they have secret conference with familiars. But in the end their familiars fall out to be a pack of knaves of their own families...
>
> Heretofore in time of Popery masters of familiars invented that the fayries haunted Butteries and Cellars, onely to make young people afraid of sitting up late in the night. Again, servants themselves sometimes would counterfeit that those Fayries used to sup in their Masters' houses, under which

colour they covered their own wanton thefts. Here hence arose that proverb in France – 'Where faire maydes are, and store of wine, the Goblins there to haunt combine.' Let a man confer with old women (for this sex is much addicted to novelties and lightness of belief) and he shall hear many strange fables of such Fayrie folks."

Such was the conduct known in Vaughan's time; it is possible to discover many sad examples of what he described.

FAIRY COUSENINGS

Firstly, from 1594, come the reports of the arrest, conviction and whipping of one Judith Philips of Bishopsgate in London. She had been involved in two separate fairy defraudings of hapless and gullible gentlefolk.

Firstly, perhaps in late 1592, Philips had become aware of a likely target, living at Upsbourne (now Upham) near Winchester in Hampshire. To seed her fraud, she buried some coins in his garden and then persuaded the wealthy farmer and his wife that marks she could discern on their foreheads disclosed that they had been chosen to receive fairy wealth. She advised them to dig under a hollow holly tree. The coins they duly found were, she told them, part of a treasure that had been disclosed to her through fairy knowledge. Philips claimed to be the daughter of a gypsy woman and a wizard father and, with magical blood flowing in her veins, she was able to perform cures and to tell fortunes.

Philips next had the farmer pay her £14 in cash, after which he was instructed to arrange a ceremony in his house to summon the fairy queen. He set out seven candlesticks, with a gold coin placed under each, and hung up his best linen sheet. The man then submitted himself to being saddled and bridled by Philips, who rode him three times around the room. Telling husband and wife that they must now lie face down on the floor whilst she went to greet her fairy majesty, Philips disappeared for a while, dressed herself up in white with a wand and then returned to the grovelling couple, whom she convinced were in the royal presence. Stunned and awed, the pair continued to lie face down in the cold for another few hours until good sense finally overcame them and they went to see what was happening – to find that their gold and linen had vanished, along with the alleged fairy medium.[264]

Back in London, Philips continued her daring dupes. She heard that a rich tripe merchant had died, leaving his widow his prosperous business and a great fortune. The story was well-known and the widow received many suitors to become her new husband. Two men, P and V, heard of her wealth and set about devising a plot to deprive her of it. P visited her home as another prospective husband and learned much of her affairs from her servants and friends. In particular, he learned that she was friendly with a Mr Grace of Essex, a lawyer who was her adviser and guide. The two men forged a letter from Mr Grace and recruited Judith Philips as their assistant. She was sent to call upon the widow, taking Grace's letter by way of introduction. Philips presented herself as a wise woman with supernatural knowledge and powers. She

264 J. Dillinger, *Magical Treasure Hunting in Europe & North America – A History*, Basingstoke: Palgrave MacMillan, 2012, 142–143.

read the widow's palm and told her facts about her affairs which it seemed impossible for a complete stranger to have known (P had picked up the gossip during his visits). Philips asked if the widow had heard rumbling sounds when she had been lying in bed. The woman had, for the two men had made noises outside the house, but Philips ascribed these to sprites around the premises.

In this way, Philips won the widow's trust. Then she told her that her late husband had hidden great quantities of gold about the house. To uncover it, she would need the help of a wise man who knew the fairy queen. Various preparations were required before he was approached. Firstly, the widow had to get together gold, rings, jewels and chains worth £100 and wind them about with yarn. This was duly done. Philips pocketed the valuables and replaced them with stones bound up in the thread. These she told the widow to lock away until her next visit. Secondly, she asked for a turkey and two capons to take to the wise man. These were provided and Philips set off towards Paddington (where apparently the fairy king and queen resided) with a maid carrying the birds. At Holborn, however, the maid was sent back to her mistress in the Shambles and Philips proceeded to an inn where she met her accomplices and divided up the stolen gold whilst they feasted upon the poultry.

Philips' new found wealth soon attracted suspicion and the authorities were alerted. A few days later, she visited the widow again, saying that she had been all that time with the fairy queen herself. To find the concealed treasure, the woman was asked to set twelve candlesticks around her house with gold and silver under each and plates laid out for them. As this was being set up, Philips was made welcome – but in the meantime the constable was called and she was caught.[265]

Much was made in the reports of this story of the naivety (and sex) of the 'tripe-wife' but both sexes and all classes were vulnerable to such duping. A trial in the court of Chancery in 1609–10 exposed another example. Thomas Rogers was the young son of a good Dorset family. He appears to have been epileptic and quite vulnerable and, in London, he fell in with Sir Anthony Ashley and his brother Saul. They realised that they could exploit Rogers' trusting nature and they had an associate of theirs called Greene contact the youth with the promise of an introduction to the fairy queen, who was interested in marriage. In order to curry favour and to ease the negotiations, Greene needed £5 or £6 in gold to give to the "fayrees." This was just one element in a much bigger plot to defraud Rogers, but it was very widely reported and may have helped inspire part of the plot of Ben Jonson's play, *The Alchemist*, in which Dapper is persuaded by Subtle to throw away his "worldly pelf" before the fairy queen can bestow new garments upon him.

A tract of 1613, describing the *Cozenages of the Wests*, describes numerous frauds by Alice West and her husband, using the device of fairy favour to trick and deprive. Their first victims were a Thomas Moore and his wife of Hammersmith, a couple whom the Wests discovered to be "well possest." Through their maid, the Wests convinced the Moores that the king and queen of faery had chosen to favour them with great riches. However, to ensure the fairies' good favour, "due

---

265 *A Quest of Enquirie, by Women to Know, Whether the Tripe Wife were Trimmed by Doll, yea or no*, 1595; *The Brideling, Sadling and Ryding of a Rich Churle in Hampshire by the Subtle Practice of one Ludeth Philips*, 1595.

rites of sacrifice" had to be undertaken first: a great banquet had to be laid on (at considerable expense) and other costly ceremonies performed. The couple and their maid were sworn to strict secrecy over these dealings, for fear that they might "not onely hazard their great fortune but incurre the danger of the fayries, and so consequently be open to great mishaps and fearfull disasters." The Moores clearly accepted that certain preparations would have to be in place to secure the fairies' approbation – and accepted too that more expense would have to be incurred when omission or mistake in the first ceremony demanded that it be repeated. All this cost the Moores £50, but it culminated in them being taken into a vault where they saw the king and queen of faerie attended by little elves and goblins and surrounded by an "infinite number" of bags (purportedly containing gold coins) upon which were written their names. They were not able to receive this wealth immediately, though. Moore finally began to doubt Alice West at this point and sought the advice of a friend. Somehow West learned of this and went to see him to warn that King Oberon was enraged that he had spoken to a third party about their secret dealings. West persuaded Moore that she was genuine and managed to get him to supply her with a large number of receptacles – chests, trunks, sacks and barrels – which she promised the fays would fill with treasure. These were provided and another meeting took place with the king and queen of faerie in a dark cellar. As much as £1,700,000 worth of riches was displayed there (according to the maid) but again the Moores could not take this wealth away as more ceremonies were necessary. West got another £80 out of Thomas Moore to pay for these – and then disappeared.

This was Alice West's most elaborate deception, but there were several others. She duped a maid servant in the Strand into sitting naked in a garden during a frosty winter's night holding a pot of earth, in the expectation that the fairy queen would turn it into gold by morning. In the meantime, West made off with the servant's clothes and savings. In another case, West told a gentlewoman that the fairy queen wished to bestow a great quantity of coin upon her. At first the woman thought it was all nonsense but, by sleight of hand, West was able to turn two one-shilling coins into twenty-shilling pieces. On this basis, the woman was enticed into parting with nearly £80 in cash in the expectation that the queen of fairies would turn every silver shilling into a gold twenty-shilling coin. West also operated from her home in Fulham, offering to tell fortunes or find lost goods for local people. She would tell her clients that the queen of fairies had told her their secrets, whereas in fact she had so set up her home that she was able to eavesdrop on the clients waiting to see her and to overhear in advance the substance of their concerns. Lastly, she defrauded a goldsmith's apprentice by telling him that the fairy queen had fallen in love with him. He was excited by this prospect and asked Alice to arrange a meeting. She said that this could be done, but that she would need four pieces of silver and a gilt plate from the apprentice's master's shop. He provided these but, instead of meeting his fairy lover, he was beaten and robbed by her accomplices. For all of these frauds West was whipped, pilloried and imprisoned.[266]

Just as the case of Thomas Rogers may have helped inspire Ben Jonson, the activities of the Wests (as well as the model of

---

266 J. O. Halliwell-Phillips, *Illustrations of the Fairy Mythology of 'A midsummer Night's Dream'*, London: Shakespeare Society, 1845, c.XII.

his forerunner) very likely gave inspiration to Robert Amin, who in 1615 produced his play, *The Valiant Welshman*. In its second act, Morion, a foolish knight, falls in love with the fairy queen and is persuaded by Juggler that it may be possible to arrange an introduction. Juggler regards the knight as an idiot and ripe for deception. Morion is told that, to come into the queen's presence, he must approach her on his hands and knees, without his doublet, cloak, hose, rapier or anything that may offend her nose. Having divested himself of all these items, they are of course stolen from the gullible knight.

Other seventeenth century examples come from Wales. A woman called Anne Jones was imprisoned in November 1634 for swindling several people in the north of the country. John Lewys, of Bryneglwys, Denbigh, had been persuaded by her that his daughter was stricken with an illness (perhaps inflicted by the fairies) which Anne could alleviate with the help of the faes and offerings to them of nine shillings in cash and a quantity of cloth. Anne had received the cash and cloth and promptly disappeared. However, only a month later, she was at Corwen, only a few miles away, where she offered to cure Griffith ap Owen's sickly child with the fairies' aid. For this, she required a substantial sum of money from him (forty-five shillings) which she needed just to 'show' to the fairies. He gave her the money and, of course, Anne vanished – but not well enough. She was traced, arrested and tried.

In 1636, a vagrant called Harry Lloyd was brought before the magistrates of Caernarfon for defrauding a farmer called John Howell of Hirdre, near Tudweiliog. Lloyd had claimed regular contact with the fairies, on Tuesday and Thursday nights, and had said that through his good offices other local men received regular sums of money from them. He now asked Howell for two shillings to buy wax so that he could make candles to give to the fairies as a sign of Howell's good will. The farmer complied, but the meeting with the fairies that followed didn't go well. Lloyd said that fairies wanted from Howell a better indication of his good will – in the form of four shillings. Lloyd received this too – and disappeared from the farm – at which point it finally dawned upon Howell that he had been duped.[267]

THE FAIRIES OF HOUNSLOW HEATH

Perhaps the most intriguing story of fairy fraud from this period is that of the Honourable Goodwin Wharton (1653– 1704), a gentleman and former Member of Parliament who had prolonged dealings with the fairies in the late seventeenth century. His story is a barely credible mixture of magic, madness and deceit.

Wharton was the younger son of an aristocratic family from Buckinghamshire. During his career, he dabbled in inventing, alchemy and the occult. In early 1683 in London, he met a woman in her early fifties called Mary Parish. She made her living as a folk healer and wise woman, selling love charms and herbal remedies. She was originally from the Chiltern village Turville, where her grandfather, a humble charcoal maker, had found a pot of fairy gold whilst digging a charcoal pit in Northend Woods. The inscription on the vessel had said there was more to be found in the locality – if only you knew where to look. In her youth, Mary had scoured

---

267 see R. Sugg, 'The Fair Folk and Enchanters,' in *Magical Folk*, 2018, 145–8.

the woods and on one occasion had stumbled upon fairies dancing in a glade. Because she plainly had second sight, her family had sent her to learn medicine with an uncle, who also taught her alchemy and the occult arts.

By the early 1680s, Parish had slipped into poverty, but then she had had a stroke of luck. Walking on Hounslow Heath one day, she heard church bells ringing under the ground and followed the sound into the Lowlands – the subterranean fairy kingdom. There she visited the royal palace and was befriended and favoured by the fairy king and queen. Hearing this account from Parish, Wharton realised that he had encountered a woman with significant powers and contacts and they entered into a partnership together – both sexual and commercial.

According to Parish, faery was a place very similar to the human world. The Hounslow Heath fairies were mortal beings but extremely long lived; they often kept their youthful good looks for a thousand years or more. To mortal eyes, they appeared to be only about three feet tall, but they were in fact of normal human size but chose to diminish themselves using magical breastplates that they wore. They could appear and disappear at will using similar magical equipment. The fairies were Roman Catholic and closely respected the rules of Mosaic Law. Lowland was ruled by King Byron and Queen Penelope LaGard. The faery court was as susceptible to intrigue and excess as any earthly one: amongst its residents were Princess Ursula LaPerle, the queen's beautiful but traitorous sister; Cottrell, the queen's wicked confessor; Father Friar, an aged counsellor and alchemist; the Duke and Duchess of Brittany; the Duke of Lorraine; and the faithless Duke of Hungary. These various characters were fairly clearly invented by Mary Parish.

As we saw earlier, none of the authentic folklore evidence gives any hint of such personages assembled at the fairy court.

Matters then began to develop quickly. In April 1683, Mary's spirit guide, an executed criminal called George, brought a message from the queen of Faery saying that she wished to visit Wharton at his home. Sadly, she twice failed to arrive, whilst on a third occasion she had found Wharton asleep and had lacked the heart to awaken him. To make up for these setbacks, Queen Penelope invited both Parish and Wharton to visit her at court on May Day. This trip had to be cancelled because the queen's period started unexpectedly and fairy custom prohibited her from seeing men at such times. The queen's 'impure' status during her period looks to be one of those Old Testament rules to which the Lowlanders were apparently subject. This facet of faery morality seems to be part of Parish's fantasy, although British fairies are known to wash regularly (frequently coming into human homes to do so) and a widespread element in spells to conjure fairies was a requirement that the magician would prepare by making himself pure in body and conduct.

There were plenty of other frustrations to follow. Parish and Wharton were regularly summoned to the court, but would then be prevented by some last-minute hitch from attending. On one occasion, they got as far as the gates of the Lowlands, only to find that they had been flooded and were impassable; on another, they travelled to Hounslow but were met by the news that King Byron had got so drunk the night before that he was in no fit state to receive them. Before too long, his alcoholism proved fatal and then – of course – all visits had to be postponed until the long period of mourning that was prescribed in fairy custom had concluded.

Although Wharton was repeatedly disappointed in his hopes of meeting the queen in person, she had seen him – and had taken a fancy to what she'd seen. Following the death of King Byron, the queen informed Wharton (through George and Mary) that she now wished to marry him and make him the new king of Faery. In fact, he had proved so irresistible to Penelope that for some weeks she had secretly visited him at night and had had sex with him whilst he was asleep. Despite his unconscious state, they had had intercourse as often as three times nightly, a revelation that for Wharton explained the tiredness and backache that had recently afflicted him. Unhappily, in the autumn George had to announce that the queen had suffered a miscarriage, losing twin boys whom Wharton had fathered. Penelope was left in very frail health and would not be able to visit Wharton again for several months. As it happened, it was just at this time that Wharton and Parish became intimate, a physical relationship that (incredibly) led to 107 pregnancies in the space of twenty years.

Despite the previous rebuffs, during the spring of 1684, Parish and Wharton made further journeys to Hounslow but enjoyed no greater success in gaining access to the queen. In due course, however, Penelope promised that she would send a coach for Wharton which would carry him to the Lowland colony at Moorfields, where the fairy pope would perform their marriage ceremony. Rather like the individual named Father Friar identified at the royal court, this pope and the suggestion that the fairies were Catholics all seem to be products of Parish's fertile imagination and a reaction to the very human religious prejudices of the period.

Yet again, the plans went awry: an accident on the road and the untimely start of the queen's period both intervened to prevent their union. The wedding was then postponed repeatedly during the rest of that year for a variety of excuses, including an attempt by the fairy Duke of Hungary to assassinate Penelope with a poisoned dish of chocolate. Nonetheless, Wharton was reassured of his position when he was told of the public announcement in Faery that confirmed him as the new king. Sadly, and before they ever met face to face (and awake), Queen Penelope died in 1686. She was succeeded by her sister Ursula, who proved just as anxious to marry Wharton as her sister had been (presumably because he was the rightful heir) but angels advised him not to succumb to her charms and he somehow resisted her attempts to seduce him, even while he was asleep. Tragically, Ursula died within a year of her sister, which somehow left Wharton as the sole and undisputed monarch of the Lowlands.

Whilst consummating his royal relationship and ascending his faery throne were proving so problematic, Parish and Wharton had had other matters to keep them occupied. They resolved to discover the remainder of the fairy gold buried in the woods at Northend. By the end of 1683, they had located the site of the treasure, which was apparently substantial. However, they had also discovered that there was an evil spirit called Rumbonium guarding the hoard. This was entirely in line with faery belief at the time. We have records of a number of spells that summon fairies into a conjurer's presence and requiring them to bring treasure with them as well as to give advice as to the location of buried riches and how to destroy any spirits set to watch over them.[268]

---

268 Manuscript MS Xd 234, Folger Library, Washington D.C.

Fortunately for the pair of treasure seekers, Mary's supernatural guide George discovered another spirit called Bromka, who was more inclined to be friendly towards them; he told them that Rumbonium was always absent from the site on Monday afternoons. Accordingly, one Monday afternoon in July 1684, Wharton and Parish travelled to Northend Wood to exhume the gold unchallenged. As they had been advised, Rumbonium wasn't present but three even more dangerous beings – named Rismin, Osmindor and Accoron – were on guard in his place. More time was lost exorcising this trio of spirits and, even when this had been accomplished, it was discovered that the treasure was too big to be removed without help. Another visit had to be arranged, in advance of which an invisible team of fairy servants were hired for fifty guineas from the Duke of Lorraine. All were present and correct when Bromka informed George that that the treasure had vanished. The prospectors only coped with this unexplained reversal of fortune because they received the news that nearby were buried the Urim and Thummim, stolen from the temple of Jerusalem in 70 AD. This fabulous prize was guarded by a spirit called Ruben Pen Dennis, who was prepared to let the pair take it away the following week. They returned seven days later only to be told by Bromka that they were fifteen minutes too late, because again the treasure has simply disappeared.

Despite her repeated failures in the Chilterns, Parish pursued other hoards of buried treasure, mainly in London. She discovered a rich treasure under a house in Ratcliffe, in the East End, but it was guarded by a spirit named Thomas Shashbesh. The subterranean passages here offered a new route to the fairy colonies at Hounslow and Moorfields, but regrettably "great monstrous serpents, snakes, and toads, which lay warbling and heaving and rolling," blocked the way.

Goodwin Wharton meanwhile, found conventional earthly success and riches. In 1690, he was once again elected to Parliament and became active and respected, with established expertise in finance and military matters. In due course, he was appointed as one of the Lords of the Admiralty. This status and respectability didn't mean that he had entirely abandoned his occult interests, nor his supernatural helpers. During the naval battle of Beachy Head, fought on July 10th 1690, he ordered his fairy subjects to steal invisibly on board the French vessels and dampen their gunpowder. With his accumulated military knowledge and experience, he also devised plans to invade his fairy kingdom. Lastly, in July 1691, Wharton travelled to Tobermory in Scotland with two naval ships to explore for sunken treasure. His expedition was seriously delayed through waiting for a fairy helper by the name of Jeffrey, who was an expert diver, and for delivery of magical breathing apparatus promised to him by angels. No treasure was found but Wharton did manage to salvage fourteen guns from the wreck, which enhanced his standing further.

This is, all in all, a very puzzling story. Wharton appears to have been a compound of naivety, greed, credulity and madness. His persistent belief in help from the fairies and angels, in the face of ceaseless disappointments, is remarkable. It would be easy to dismiss him as a fool, were it not for the fact that his public service demonstrates he was capable and clever. Very evidently, Mary Parish had some strong hold over him, not just with her tales of fairies and gold but with her multiple and frequent pregnancies; he seems to have accepted her prodigious fecundity as well as her inability to present him with a single live child. The fifty guineas she obtained to pay to the fairy Duke of Lorraine must give some inkling of what she gained from all of this – as well, perhaps, as the unquestioning devotion of a younger man.

It will be apparent from this last example that anyone, in any class, might be victim to fairy fraud. It was not solely the poor and the desperate – nobles, successful entrepreneurs, both men and woman, all might succumb. The same was true of intellectuals, too. William Lilly, a researcher into the occult and magic, made many experiments to summon the fairy queen into his presence. As he ruefully recorded in his autobiography, his active engagement in this work attracted to him many fraudsters who pretended to be able to summon Queen Mab, but who were unable actually to do so. Doubtless, their motivation was to gain from the credulous Lilly if they might.[269]

LATER EXAMPLES

By no means are these stories solely the product of Tudor and Stuart times. For example, during the eighteenth century along the Welsh-English border, highwaymen found that a good way of stealing horses was to pretend to have heard fairy music. They would lie on the ground by the road, ear pressed to the earth, and when a rider came by, they would regularly dismount, first to offer help and then to lie down to hear the fairy music too.[270]

---

269 Lilly, *Autobiography*, 271.
270 Jacqueline Simpson, *Folklore of the Welsh Border*, 1976, 50; *Notes and Queries*, series 4, volume 9, 135.

In 1818, a case was heard before Marlborough Street police court, in which a fortune teller called Elizabeth Hay was accused of fraud by a domestic servant, Mary Woodward. Hay had approached Woodward in the street and persuaded her (and the daughter of her employers) that the house in which they lived had been constructed upon fairy ground. She persuaded them that, if they dropped a red and a blue liquid in the yard behind the house at four each afternoon, a buried fairy treasure would be revealed to them. On the basis that they would soon find £600, Hay managed to extort money and clothes from Woodward over a three-week period. The latter finally became suspicious, at which point Hay vanished. It was her very bad luck to be spotted in Marylebone two years later, otherwise she might have got away with her imposture.[271]

Fairy frauds continued to be successful as late as the last quarter of the nineteenth century. In 1872, a woman from Scarborough was charged with obtaining money under false pretences from a fellow domestic servant. The accused had told her companion that she had the power to cure illness caused by a hostile spell, an ability she had acquired as a result of her connection with Lord Fell, king of the fairies. A crueller example of this same deceit was practised by an old woman from County Cork; Mary Keefe. In 1868, she appeared before Rivertown petty sessions charged with obtaining money from Mary Murray on the pretence that she had regular contact with the fairies and could, through them, find a cure for Murray's sickly child. [272]

---

271 R. Sugg, *Fairies – A Dangerous History,* London: Reaktion Books, 2018, 70–71.

272 *County Observer,* August 8th 1868, 2.

In 1880 in Sheffield, an elderly woman, Agnes Johnstone, was jailed for three weeks for having obtained £5 8/– by deception from Margaret Devaney. The details of the offence closely resemble those from centuries earlier. Agnes read Devaney's fortune and told her that she could "rule the planet" so long as she provided some money to help secure the inheritance that was due to her. Johnstone received sums over a period of time, saying that she was regularly in touch with the fairies, who had danced before her, and that she was working with the devil. She added that the fairies would be bringing Devaney her fortune, which would be delivered to her by underground passages. A Leeds housemaid proved just as gullible nearly two decades later. Margaret Rohan, aged 38, had come to the house where Lily Holmes was employed, offering to mend umbrellas. There were none needing attention, but she then said she'd read Lily's fortune for sixpence. Lily was promised great wealth, provided she supplied money and some items of clothing for Rohan to bury. She took these items, and allegedly interred them, but then came back for more cash to give to the "life fairies" who were like flies and came out at night. She got more silver – and then wasn't seen again.[273]

An interesting twist upon this theme was heard by Carlisle Quarter Sessions in October 1860. Daniel O'Hara and his wife were charged with receiving fourteen gold sovereigns that had been stolen by their daughter from the house in Whitehaven where she worked as a maid. The girl told her parents that she had found the coins, some hidden in ashes, some in a basket. To this, her father replied that "tha little fairies had likely sent

---

273 *Weekly Mail*, Nov 13th 1880, 8– 'Fortune and the Fairies;' *South Wales Echo*, January 12th 1897, 2– 'A Credulous Servant Girl.'

them," and he had advised his daughter not to speak about the money again, because that way more might come. Upon his arrest, O'Hara told the police that he had often seen the fairies by the fire, counting the money, before they flew up the chimney. The family used to leave out milk and tobacco for them. Mr O'Hara's genuine belief in the fairies was accepted by the court and his credulity spared him jail, whereas his wife was sentenced to twelve months with hard labour.[274]

OTHER TYPES OF FRAUD

A credulous belief in fairies can be exploited by the unscrupulous in other ways. In times past, travelling freak shows were a frequent part of fairs and circuses and fairy exhibits were a common attraction in these.

At Bartholomew Fair in the early nineteenth century, you could aspire to see the following:

> "a living elf, supposed to be 150 years old, his face being no bigger than a child's of a month; was found 60 years ago; looked as old then as he does now. His head being a great piece of curiosity, having no skull…"

Another handbill of about the same time advertised a fairy child that could be seen at a fair held at the Black Raven Tavern in West Smithfield, London:

---

274 'Fairies Implicated in a Robbery,' *Illustrated Usk & Raglan Observer*, October 27th 1860, 3.

"aged nine years and a month, not exceeding one and a half feet high. The legs, thighs and arms so very small, that they scare exceed the bigness of a man's thumb, and the face no bigger than the palm of one's hand; seems so grave and solid as if we three score years old. It never speaks. It has no teeth but is the most voracious and hungry creature in the world, devouring more victuals than the stoutest man in England."

Evidently these were severely disabled people, possibly not infants, effectively imprisoned by the fairs. Their chronic disabilities and deformities echoed the descriptions of fairy changelings known from popular tradition and gave verisimilitude to the deception.

CONCLUSIONS

It is noteworthy that fairy frauds are not restricted to Britain. In Ireland, particularly focussed during the Great Famine of the mid-nineteenth century, there was an outbreak of fairy-related impostures. An analysis of these has revealed that the majority of perpetrators were female, as seems to have been the case in Britain too, whilst the necessary personal traits required of a successful fairy fraudster are reckoned to have included a 'swindling personality', that is, the daring and calmness to carry off the trick, combined with a good knowledge of fairy lore and beliefs relating to the dead. The ability to identify likely victims, and to exploit their weak spots, might be added to this.[275]

---

275 Simon Young, *Fairy Impostures in the Great Famine*, 2019, *Academia. com.*

That any of these deceptions could succeed at all demonstrates to us how strongly held fairy beliefs were in the past, even in urban areas and relatively recently. Not just the existence of the faeries was taken for granted, but their access to considerable wealth and their willingness to share it with certain chosen humans. So embedded were these ideas that (combined with greed) it seemed possible for some persuasive individuals to get away with almost any imposture.

Conclusion: The Fairy Economy Analysed

What can we make of the fairy economy? How does it function?

The popular view of fairies is that they are a pleasure loving and indulgent people who give their time over to feasting, drinking and pastimes such as music, riding, hunting and sport. The bulk of the sightings see them involved in just such activities. As I have enumerated, witnesses have also seen them cultivating and manufacturing, but these instances are far fewer. Taking these figures at face value, the implication is that there are simply not enough fairies spending sufficient time to make all the goods, cutlery, plates and clothes they use, nor to grow adequate supplies of food, to satisfy their basic needs – let alone to cater for their conspicuous consumption.

At first glance, then, the fairy economy is imbalanced and cannot function effectively; there ought to be starvation and want – and perhaps the cases of borrowing goods and comestibles are evidence of exactly this. However, as I have already demonstrated, there is another element to the fairy economy – and that is the asset represented by humans. The fairies are able to exist (and to have time for entertainment) because much of their produce – and their labour – comes from us.

As we have seen, the faes can buy – or they can steal – human resources. The legitimate acquisition of human goods and services potentially raises another problem – that of ready cash. If fairy productivity is inadequate even for their own needs, and if their contact with human kind is limited in any case, they cannot make or grow enough to sell to us to generate an income with which they can buy other goods. This would – in the mortal world – be a major problem, but luckily the faes have supernatural access to hidden gold and other treasure, meaning that they may never run out of ready money to pay for food or for midwives. This argument assumes, of course, an inclination to bargain legitimately for the things they want. As we've also discussed, such an impulse is far weaker amongst fairykind than the inclination simply to take what they want. Equipped as they are with the magical powers of invisibility and glamour, it's easy enough for the faes to take all the livestock, dairy products and grain they wish – and folklore affirms that they do just this. Secondly, abductions of humans to act as musicians and domestic drudges for their communities free the supernatural population to enjoy themselves. Stark confirmation of this habit comes from Glen Errochty in Perthshire. A local seer there was asked by a widow where her husband was; doubtless she wondered if he was in heaven or hell and she was probably horrified to learn that, "He is a baggage horse to the Fairies in Slevach Cairn, with a twisted willow with in his mouth." The Cairn was notorious in the locality as a *sithean,* a fairy hill, and the late husband was not dead – as had appeared – but had been taken and bridled by the 'Good Folk.'[276]

Whilst mentioning these abductions, a few remarks ought to be made about the size of the fairy population. They are known to be very long lived, although probably not immortal. This being so, there is plainly the potential for a continuing and escalating crisis of more and more mouths to feed and bodies to dress. Fairy births take place – we know that from the accounts of midwives abducted – yet the indications are that the birth rate is not high in Faery. This may partly account for the taking of human infants, who would obviously contribute no useful labour for some time and yet would need to be fed and cared for. From what we can gather, there would appear to be a static population in Faery, from which it follows that the pressure for resources is not as great as we might have anticipated. Secondly, whilst the changeling phenomenon may add infants to their population, we should not overlook the fact that the 'changeling' left in a human household in exchange will be an elderly fairy – not infrequently with a voracious appetite. The burden of personal care and feeding the fairy cuckoo is cunningly shifted to the fairies' human neighbours, saving considerably for them.

In summary, how may we describe the fairy economy? I think it's not unfair to regard it as parasitic upon humankind, a form of cynical colonial exploitation of assets and resources. Without the unwilling and unwitting input from the human world, the fairy way of life might be unsustainable; certainly, it would involve a great deal more hard graft on their part.

---

276 Campbell, *Superstitions*, 94.

Instead, by sponging off the ingenuity and toil of their mortal neighbours, the fairies are able to subsidise a leisured lifestyle for themselves. They hold economic sway over us and, with their magical powers, we can do almost nothing about it.

Bibliography

Addy, Sidney. *Household Tales.* London: Nutt, 1895;

Aitken, Hannah. *A Forgotten Heritage – Original Folk Tales of Lowland Scotland.* Scottish Academic Press, 1973;

Anon, *A Pleasant Treatise of Witches.* London: C. Wilkinson, Thomas Archer and Thomas Burrell.1673;

Anon, *A Quest of Enquirie, by Women to Know, Whether the Tripe Wife were Trimmed by Doll, yea or no.* 1595;

Anon, 'Collecteanea,' *Folklore,* vol.25, 1913;

Anon. *Folklore and Legends: Scotland.* W. W. Gibbings, 1889;

Anon, *Legends of Scottish Superstition.* Edinburgh: W. & H. Robinson, 1848;

Anon, *The Brideling, Sadling and Ryding of a Rich Churle in Hampshire by the Subtle Practice of one Ludeth Philips.* 1595;

Anon, *The Pranks of Puck.* c.1628;

Archaeologia Cambrensis, vol.3, 1886;

Aubrey, J. *Remains of Gentilism.* London: Folklore Society, 1881;

Natural History of Surrey, 1718, vol.3;

Bailey, J. *Lancashire Folk Tales.* Stroud: The History Press, 2014;

Barton, I. *North Yorkshire Folk Tales.* Stroud: The History Press, 2014;

Baxter, R. *The Certainty of the World of Spirits.* London: Parkhurst & Salisbury, 1691;

Beaumont & Fletcher, *The Honest Man's Fortune.* 1613;

Billingsley, John. *West Yorkshire Folk Tales*. Stroud: The History Press, 2010;

Black, D. *History of Brechin*. Brechin: W. Patterson, 1839;

Blakeborough, R. *Wit, Character, Folklore & Customs of the North Riding of Yorkshire: With a Glossary of over 4,000 Words and Idioms Now in Use*. London: Henry Frowde, 1898;

Blight, J. T. *A Week at Land's End*, Truro: Lake and Lake, 1876;

Bord, Janet. *Fairies – Real Encounters with Little People*. New York: Carroll & Graf, 1997;

Bottrell, William. *Traditions and Hearthside Stories of West Cornwall*. Penzance, volume 1, 1870 and volume 2, 1873;

Bovet, R. *Pandaemonium*, London: J. Walthoe, 1684;

Bowker, James. *Goblin Tales of Lancashire*. London: Swan Sonnenschein, 1878;

Boyd, H. *Poems*, Dublin: Graisberry & Campbell, 1793;

Brand, John. *A Description of Zetland*. Edinburgh: W. Brown, 1883;

Bray, Anna. *Peeps on Pixies*. London: Grant and Griffith, 1854;

Briggs, Katherine. "The Fairy Economy – As it May be Deduced from a Group of Folk Tales", *Folklore*, vol. 70 (1959);

"English Fairies", *Folklore*, vol.68;

Dictionary of Fairies, Penguin, 1977;

Folk Tales and Legends: A Sampler. 1977;

Broome, D. *Fairy Tales from the Isle of Man*. Douglas: NMP Books, 1968;

More Fairy Tales from the Isle of Man, Douglas: NMP Books, 1970;

Browne, James. *History of the Highlands*. Glasgow: A. Fullerton & Co, 1838;

Browne, W. *The Shepherd's Pipe*, 1614;

Burne, C. 'Staffordshire Folk and Their Lore', *Folklore*, vol.7, 1896;

Bye Gones, 1882–83;

Campbell, J. F. *Popular Tales of the West Highlands.* Edinburgh: Edmonston & Douglas, vol.2, 1860;

Waifs and Strays of Celtic Tradition. London: Nutt, 1895, vol.5, (Argyllshire Series);

Campbell, J. G *Superstitions of the Highlands & Islands.* Glasgow: James MacLehose & Sons, 1900;

Cargill Guthrie, J. *The Vale of Strathmore,* Edinburgh: W. Paterson, 1875;

Carmichael, Alexander. *Carmina Gadelica.* Edinburgh: Oliver & Boyd, vol.2. 1900;

Celtic Monthly, vol.IV, 1895;

Chapman, G. *A Humorous Day's Mirth,* 1597;

Choice Notes & Queries – Folklore, London, 1859;

Churchyard, T. *A Handful of Gladsome Verses,* 1593;

Clinton-Baddeley, V. C. *Dartmoor,* London: A&C Black, 1925;

Cobb, W. W. 'Anglesey Folklore, from near Holyhead,' *Y Cymmrodor,* 1886, vol.7;

Cope, Elijah.*Memorials of Old Staffordshire.* London: George, Allen & Unwin, 1909;

Couch, J. *History of Polperro,* Truro: W. Lake, 1871;

County Folklore, London: The Folklore Society, 190 1–1965:

Somerset, vol.8;

County Folklore vol.7;

Courtney, Margaret. *Cornish Feasts and Folklore.* Penzance: Beare & Son, 1890;

Cowper, Henry. *Hawkshead.* London: Bemrose & Sons, 1899;

Coxhead, J. *Devon Traditions and Fairy Tales.* Exmouth: Deiderfield & Sons, 1959;

Crofton Croker, Thomas. *Fairy Legends and Traditions.* London: John Murray, vol.3, 1828;

Cromek, R. *Remains of Nithsdale & Galloway Song*, London: Cadell & Davies, 1910;

Crossing, William. *Tales of Dartmoor Pixies*. Newcastle upon Tyne: F. Graham, 1890;

Daimler, M. *A New Dictionary of Fairy – A 21st Century Exploration of Celtic and Related Western European Fairies*. Andover: Moon Publications, 2020;

Dalyell, John. *The Darker Superstitions of Scotland*. Edinburgh: Waugh & Innes,1834;

Deane, Tony & Shaw, Tony. *Folklore of Cornwall*. Stroud: The History Press, 2009;

Dempster, 'Folklore of Sutherlandshire,' *Folklore Journal*, vol.6, 1888;

Dillinger, J. *Magical Treasure Hunting in Europe & North America – A History*, Basingstoke: Palgrave MacMillan, 2012;

Dixon, *Pitlochry Past & Present*, Pitlochry:L. Mackay, 1925;

Doel, *Folklore of Northumberland*, Stroud: The History Press Ltd, 2009;

Douglas, G. *Scottish Fairy & Folk Tales*, New York: A. L. Burt Company, 1901;

Drayton, M. *Nymphidia*, 1627;

Emerson, 'The Ploughman and the Fairies,' *Folklore*, vol.7, 1896;

Evans-Wentz, Walter. *The Fairy Faith in Celtic Countries*. Oxford: Oxford University Press,1911;

Fletcher, J. *Rule a Wife*, 1624;

Fletcher, J. *The Faithful Shepherdess*, 1608-9;

Forsyth, W. *The Shadow of Cairngorm*, Inverness: The Northern Counties Publishing Company, Ltd., 1900;

Gill, Walter. *A Manx Scrapbook*. London: Arrowsmith, 3 volumes, 1929 & 1932;

Glanvill, J. *Saducismus Triumphatus*, London, 1668;

Gomme, (ed.), *Gentleman's Magazine Library,* 1885;

Gomme, A. 'Collectanea: Harvest Customs,' *Folklore,* vol.13, 1902;

Goodrich-Freer, A. 'The Powers of Evil in the Outer Hebrides,' *Folklore,* vol.10, 1899;

Graham, D. *The History of Buckhaven.* Stirling: W. Macnie, 1779;

Grant Stewart, William. *The Popular Superstitions and Festive Amusements of the Highlanders of Scotland.* London: Aylott & Jones, 1823;

Gregor, Walter. *Notes on the Folklore of the North East of Scotland.* London;

Folklore Society, 1881;

"A Sketch of Scottish Diablerie in General," *Fraser's Magazine,* vol.25 (1842);

HGT, 'Pixies or Pisgies, *Notes & Queries,* 1850, no.61;

Haldane-Burgess, J. 'Some Shetland Folklore,' *Scottish Review,* vol.25, 1895;

Halliwell, James. *Illustrations of the Fairy Mythology of A Midsummer Night's Dream.* London: Shakespeare Society, 1845;

Hancock, F. *The Parish of Selworthy.* 1877;

Harrison, W. *Historical Description of the Island of Britain.* London, 1577;

Hawker, R. *Footprints of Former Men in Far Cornwall.* London: John Lane,1893;

Henderson, G. *Popular Rhymes, Sayings & Proverbs of the County of Berwick.* Newcastle: W S Crow, 1856;

Heron, R. *Observations Made in a Journey.* Perth: W. Morison, and Glasgow: John Murdoch, 1799;

Hewison, *The Isle of Bute in Olden Time.* Edinburgh and London, William Blackwood and Sons, 1893;

Hewlett, M. *The Lore of Proserpine.* New York: Charles Scribner, 1913;

Heyrick, T. *The New Atlantis.* 1687;

Heywood, T. *Hierarchie of Blessed Angels,* London, 1635;

Hill, Paul. *Folklore of Northamptonshire.* Stroud: The History Press, 2005;

Horne, J. *The County of Caithness,* Wick: W. Rae, 1907;

Hunt, Robert. *Popular Romances of the West of England.* London: Chatto & Windus, 1903;

Jenkinson, Henry. *A Practical Guide to the Isle of Man.* London: E. Stanford, 1874;

Jenkyn Thomas, William. *Welsh Fairy Book.* New York: F. A. Stokes, 1908;

Johnson, Marjorie. *Seeing Fairies.* San Antonio: Anomalist Books, 2014;

Johnson, S. *A Journey to the Western Isles of Scotland.* Edinburgh: Lawrie & Symington, 1774;

Jones, Edmund. *The Appearance of Evil – Apparitions of Spirits in Wales.* Cardiff: University of Wales Press, 2003;

Jones, G. 'Y Tylwyth Teg,' *Llen Cymru,* vol.8, 1965;

Jones, William. *Credulities of the Past.* London: Catto & Windus, 1880;

Jonson, B. *Eastward Ho!* 1605;

Jonson, B. *The Silent Woman.* 1609;

Keightley, Thomas. *The Fairy Mythology.* London: G. Bell, 1850;

Kirk, R. *Secret Commonwealth*;

Leather, E. *Folklore of Herefordshire.* Hereford: Jakeman & Carver, 1912;

Leney, I. H. *Shadowland in Ellan Vannin.* London: Elliott Stock, 1890;

Lewes, Mary. *Stranger Than Fiction.* London: Rider & Son, 1911;

Lilly, J. *Autobiography,* London, 1715;

Lyndsay, D. *Complaynt of the Papingo,* 1529;

MacCulloch, E. *Guernsey Folklore,* London: Elliott Stock, 1903;

Macdiarmid, J. 'Fragments of Breadalbane Folklore,' *Transactions of the Gaelic Society of Inverness,* vol.26, 1905;

MacDougall James & Calder George. *Folk Tales and Fairy Lore in Gaelic and English.* Edinburgh: John Grant, 1910;

Macgregor, Alasdair. *The Peat Fire Flame: Folk Tales and Traditions of the Highlands and Islands.* Edinburgh: Moray Press,1937;

MacKenzie, D. *The Book of Arran.* Arran: Kilbrannan Publishing, 1914;

MacKenzie, Donald. *Wonder Tales from Scottish Myths.* London: Blackie & Sons, 1917;

Manx Notes & Queries;

Marwick, Ernest. *The Folklore of Orkney and Shetland.* Edinburgh: Birlinn Ltd, 2011;

Mathews, F. *Tales of the Blackdown Borderland.* Taunton: Somerset Folk Press, 1923;

McArthur, *Antiquities of Arran.* Edinburgh: Adam, Charles & Black, 1873;

McCulloch, J. 'Folklore of the Isle of Skye,' *Folklore,* vol. 34, 1922;

McPhail, M. 'Hebrides Folklore,' *Folklore,* vol.11, 1900;

Macdonald, A. 'A Witchcraft Case of 1647,' *Scots Law Times,* April 10th, 1937;

MacPhail, J. *Highland Papers.* Edinburgh: T. and A. Constable for the Scottish History Society, 1914–34;

Marshall, T. H. *The History of Perth,* Perth: J. Fisher, 1849;

Martin, M. *A Description of the Western Isles of Scotland,* London: Andrew Bell, 1716;

Milne, John. *Myths & Superstitions of the Buchan District.* R. Jack, 1891;

Monteath, J. *Dunblane Traditions,* Glasgow: John Miller, 1887;

Montgomerie, *Flyting Between Montgomerie & Polwart.* 1515;

Moore, Arthur. *Folklore of the Isle of Man.* London: D. Nutt, 1891;

Morrison, Sophia, 'Manx Dialect Connected with Fairies', *Proceedings of the Isle of Man Natural History and Archaeological Society,* New Series vol.1, 1906;

Manx Fairy Tales. London: D. Nutt, 1911;

Murray, Lady Evelyn. *Tales from Highland Perthshire,* 'Gaelic texts no.7.' Edinburgh: Scottish Gaelic Texts Society, 2009;

Narvaez, Peter. *The Good People – New Fairylore Essays.* Lexington: University of Kentucky Press,1997;

Nashe, *Pierce Pennilesse,* 1592;

New Statistical Accounts of Scotland, Edinburgh & London: W. Blackwood & Sons, 1845;

Nicolson, J. *Shetland Folklore.* London: R. Hale, 1981;

Northcote, R. 'Devonshire Folklore', *Folklore,* vol.11, 1900;

Notes & Queries, vol.9, 1860;

Old Lore Miscellany, Orkney and Shetland, vol.3, 1909;

Owen, E. 'Folklore Superstitions, Part 4,' *Collections Historical and Archaeological Regarding Montgomeryshire,* vol.18, 1885;

Welsh Folklore. Oswestry: Woodall, Minshall & Co, 1896;

Palmer, K. *Folklore of Somerset,* London: Harper Collins, 1976;

Palmer, Roy. *Folklore of Hereford and Worcester.* Hereford: Logaston Press, 1992;

Palmer, Roy. *Folklore of Worcestershire.* Hereford: Logaston Press, 2005;

Palmer, Roy. *Folklore of Gloucestershire.* Stroud: Tempus, 2001;

Pearse Chope, R. 'Folklore of Devon,' in *London Devonian Yearbook.* 1910;

Pennant, T. *A Tour in Scotland & a Voyage to the Hebrides (1772),* London: B. White, 1790;

Pitcairn's Ancient Criminal Trials in Scotland, (3 volumes) Edinburgh: William Tait, 1833;

Ralph of Coggeshall, *Chronicon Anglicanum;*

Reports and Transactions of the Devonshire Association, vol.8, 1876;

Rhys, John. *Celtic Folklore.* Oxford: Clarendon Press, 1901;

Ritchie G. & Harman M., *Exploring Scotland's Heritage: Argyll.* London: HMSO, 1985;

Roberts, Kai. *Folklore of Yorkshire.* Stroud: History Press, 2013;

Robertson, 'Folklore from the West of Ross-shire,' *Transactions of the Gaelic Society of Inverness,* vol.26, 1905;

Robin Goodfellow: His Mad Prankes and Merry Jests. London,1628;

Roeder, Charles. *Manx Folk Tales.* Isle of Man: Chiollagh Books, 1993;

Saxby, Jessie. *Shetland Traditional Lore.* Edinburgh: Grant & Murray, 1932;

Scot, Reginald. *The Discoverie of Witchcraft* (1584). London: Elliot Stock, 1886;

Sikes, Wirt. *British Goblins.* London: Sampson Low, 1880;

Simpson, Evelyn. *Folklore in Lowland Scotland.* London: J. M. Dent, 1908;

Simpson, J. *Folklore of the Welsh Border.* London: Harper Collins, 1976;

Snell, F. J. *Book of Exmoor.* London: Methuen, 1903;

Spalding Club Miscellany, vol.1, Part 3;

Spence L. *The Fairy Tradition in Britain.* London: Rider & Co, 1948;

Sternberg, Thomas. *Dialect and Folklore of Northamptonshire.* London: J. R. Smith, 1851;

Stewart, G. *Shetland Fireside Tales.* Lerwick: T & J Manson, 1923;

Stoddard, *Remarks on local scenery & manners in Scotland during the years 1799 and 1800*. London: William Miller, 1801;

Sugg, R. 'The Fair Folk and Enchanters,' in Young, *Magical Folk*. 2018;

Sugg, R. *Faeries – A Dangerous History*. London: Reaktion Books, 2018;

Sutherland, George. *Folklore Gleanings & Character Sketches from the Far North*. Wick: John O'Groats Journal,1937;

Taylor, Lea & Troon, Sylvia. *Midlothian Folk Tales*. Stroud: History Press, 2018;

Tongue, Ruth. *Somerset Folklore*. London: Folklore Society, 1965;

Tozer, Elias. *Devonshire & Other Original Poems*. Exeter: Devon Weekly Times, 1873;

Train, Joseph. *A Historical and Statistical Account of the Isle of Man*. Douglas: M. Quiggin, 1845;

Tregarthen, Enys. *Pixie Folklore & Legends*. New York: Gramercy Books, 1996;

Folklore Tales (ed. S. Young), 2020;

Waldron, George. *A Description of the Isle of Man*. Douglas: Manx Society, 1731;

Watson, E. C. 'Celtic Mythology,' *Celtic Review*, vol.5, 1908;

Wherry, 'Miscellaneous Notes from Monmouthshire,' *Folklore*, vol.16, 1905;

Wilkie, J. *Bygone Fife, North of the Lomonds*. Edinburgh & London: William Blackwood & Sons, 1938;

Winchester, H.S. *Traditions of Arrochar and Tarbet and the Macfarlanes*. Glasgow, 1916;

Wood, J. M. *Witchcraft & Superstitious Record in South West Scotland*. E.P. Publishing, 1975;

Y Cymmrodor, vol.9, 1886;

Yn Lioar Manninagh, 1895–1901;

Young, S. 'Fairy Impostures in the Great Famine,' 2019, *Academia.com*;

Young, S. & Houlbrook, C. *Magical Folk.* London: Gibson Square, 2018.